Bloom

N.R. Walker

Copyright

Cover Artist: N.R. Walker
Editor: Boho Edits
Publisher: BlueHeart Press
Bloom © 2024 N.R. Walker

All Rights Reserved:

Warning:

Intended for an 18+ audience only. This book contains graphic language and adult situations, and is intended for a mature audience.

Trademarks:

BLURB

Keats McCulloch opened his florist shop in Sydney two years ago and he's living his dream. Even though running his own business leaves little room for a personal life, he is very single, sometimes lonely, but otherwise happy.

Linden Acres has sworn off men for all eternity. Armed with his cheating boyfriend's credit card and a floriography list, he decides to buy him the perfect farewell gift. The biggest, prettiest bouquet of 'murder flowers' his money can buy.

Keats convinces Linden to avoid possible jail time and go with a more subdued, somewhat passive aggressive bouquet of black roses and basil leaves. After all, nothing else says *you're dead to me and I hate you* with such elegance.

Keats finds Linden hilarious and charming, and Linden thinks Keats is kind of wonderful . . . It's too bad he's sworn off men forever. Yet their paths cross again and again, as if fate was planting seeds in the hope that one will bloom.

"I'm more of a green carnations kind of guy."

N.R. WALKER

BLOOM

CHAPTER ONE
KEATS McCULLOCH

TODAY WAS GOING TO BE A GREAT DAY.

I pulled the van up at work just after seven in the morning and got out. It was a brisk spring Monday in Sydney. The sky was blue, the air clean and crisp. Not even the crowded hustle at the flower markets or the stoic faces of office workers trudging to work in the city could deter my mood.

I just *knew* today was going to be a great day.

No sooner had I opened the rear doors of the van to begin unloading my haul than the back door to my shop opened and Lina and Robbie appeared.

"Morning," Lina said cheerfully.

Robbie put a coffee cup in my hand. "Morning," he said, taking a crate of flowers from the back. "Market busy?"

"Always." I sipped my coffee and sighed. "Thanks."

He smiled as he carried the box inside. "No problem."

We went about our usual morning routine: unpack the delivery, take our daily order sheets, and get to work.

My florist shop was located right in the middle of Sydney's central business district. Great foot traffic, perfect visibility, and some fantastic coffee shops and cafés close by.

Bloom was my baby. I'd worked hard to make my shop the successful business it was. It had been a hard and stressful start, but two years in and things were now very comfortable.

Robbie and Lina had been with me from the start, and I adored them both. Lina was in her early forties with her dark hair in a permanent ponytail. She was a hard worker with a cool demeanour and a contagious smile. Nothing fazed her at all.

Robbie was an astute florist with an eye for flair and a penchant for the dramatic. He was the same age as me, and I'd even go so far as to call him a close friend.

I didn't have many friends. I'd been so busy . . .

Robbie, on the other hand, had a gazillion. He had a great social life and a wonderful boyfriend.

I didn't have either of those.

My shop had been my life for the past few years. And I was okay with that. I was proud of my little florist shop, and I was proud of myself for realising my dream. I was thirty years old, and not many folks my age could say they'd accomplished their dream goals.

Aside from the loneliness that sometimes plagued me, I was very happy.

And today was going to be a good day. I could feel it. A good week, even.

Around two o'clock in the afternoon, when most of the orders were out for delivery, I was manning the desk when a guy walked in. He was in his mid-twenties, at a guess. He was kinda short, maybe five five, with chocolate brown hair, even darker eyes, and tanned skin. He had a bit of a beard happening. He wore high-end grey-blue pants with a white shirt that looked expensive.

And he came in on a mission.

"Hi," I said from behind the counter.

He smiled, showing me perfect teeth, and yeah, wow. He was really kinda gorgeous.

"Is there anything I can help you with?"

"Yes. I need some flowers," he said, referring to a list on his phone. "Uh, angel's trumpet, wolfsbane, and foxglove." His big bright eyes and pleasant smile threw me off guard for a moment. "Please."

What the hell?

"Uh, well, no. They're . . . you can't have those . . . because those are . . . those are the *bad* flowers."

He made a face. "I thought you'd say that." He went back to his list. "Any chance of a stinging tree? Some people call it a gympie-gympie or a—" He made a face. "—suicide tree, which is probably not the nicest—"

"What did this person do to you?"

"Pardon?"

"You have a fairly specific list there," I said, nodding to the phone in his hand, kinda horrified, kinda curious. "Did they kill your dog or your grandma? Because a stinging tree makes people beg for death. For years. And there is no antidote or relief. It's ongoing misery that generally leads people to opt out. Hence the name *suicide tree*."

He sighed. "I don't want him to touch it. I just want him to get the message."

"Right. I mean, sure, but it's still a no."

"And I don't want him to ingest the wolfsbane or angel's trumpets. But he's well versed in these things and he'd know which feelings I'm portraying."

I nodded slowly. "I think it's pretty clear, yeah."

"To answer your question, he's my lying, cheating, piece-of-shit, soon-to-be ex-boyfriend. And he asked me to find some flowers for his work, so it's a work expense for his business, which means he'd technically be paying for his own insult."

"Sounds fair."

He nodded. "So I googled which flowers I thought would be most appropriate."

"The ones that can injure, maim, and kill?"

He looked at the list again. "Well, I originally thought a cactus, but according to floriography, a cactus represents endurance." He winced and shook his head sadly. "Believe me, he has the opposite of that. Is there any such flower that's the opposite of endurance?"

I found myself smiling at him. "Floriographically speaking, I don't think there is."

He sighed, deflated. "That's unfortunate."

"So, let me get this straight. He's your soon-to-be ex, he's a lying, cheating piece of shit, and he lacks endurance." I nodded slowly. "I'm going to assume that you're not referring to playing a sport in which he cheats and his endurance is how long he can play this said sport, correct?"

"Correct. If I'd asked if there's a flower that says, 'You should have kept your pants zipped up,' then we'd all be on the same page."

I laughed. "Right. Well, yes. The foxglove makes sense now."

He brightened. "So can I—"

"No."

Now he pouted. "He doesn't know I know that he's a lying, cheating sack of . . . lack of endurance. But I'm thinking with an artfully chosen arrangement, he'll put the pieces together."

"So if the murder flowers are out of the question, what else are you thinking?"

He went back to his phone, quickly scrolling. "Ooh, okay.

So, according to floriography of Victorian times, black dahlias are for betrayal."

I was still smiling at him. "A bold choice." I glanced around the showroom. "Unfortunately, I don't have any in stock. They'd be a specific order."

"Snapdragons mean lies and deception. That could work."

"I have those." I thought I'd offer some suggestions. "Orange lilies are for hatred, and the negative meaning of the red tulip symbolises aggression, anger, danger, and wrath. So those are options."

He sighed, contemplating this. "I think I'm past the anger now, and I'm more into the you're-a-lying-sack-of-shit stage." He shrugged. "Aren't there flowers that smell like a rotting corpse or something? I think I read that somewhere."

I laughed again. "I believe so, yes. But again, you can't buy those. Not here at least. You'd probably need to seek out a supplier online, and maybe a permit?"

He sighed dramatically. "Okay, so no murder flowers, no rotting-corpse flowers. This isn't much fun."

I was still smiling at him. "I'm sure we can find a middle ground. Are we talking one bouquet or a centrepiece?"

"It's for the reception desk in his salon, Vintage Emporium. He said you've done arrangements for him before."

Ah. I knew that place. Very upmarket, and the owner was a douche. I assumed we were talking about the same guy. "Right, yes. I am familiar with it. From memory, I think there was one large arrangement for the reception and one smaller arrangement for the waiting area."

He produced a credit card from his pocket. "Probably. It doesn't matter. Charge him double."

I chuckled. "Well, I won't do that. But how about we work out some more details on the flowers?"

"Sure. As long as it's a clear message."

I couldn't help but like this guy. "For what it's worth, I'm sorry he hurt you."

His face softened for a second, and in that moment, the hardness in his eyes melted and I saw maybe a glimpse of the real him. "I am too," he murmured. Then his gaze hardened again. "And I'd like him to be *really* sorry, but you won't let me buy the murder flowers."

I laughed. "Okay, but I'm thinking something like this might work." I began putting a few flowers together. "What about some hydrangea, which is supposed to mean *heartless*," I said. "Surrounded by black basil leaves, which according to old Victorian times means *I hate you*."

Now he smiled. "I think we're onto something here."

"Then for the larger piece, we can reverse the colours," I suggested. "Green carnations on the outside with black roses in the centre."

He scanned the list on his phone again, then looked up and smiled at me with his hand to his heart. "Green carnations mean *homosexuality* and black roses mean *you're dead to me*. So black roses surrounded by green carnations would mean *you're dead to me, you big old homosexual*, and I think that's beautiful." He sighed. "Poetry with flowers."

I laughed. "Are you sure he'll get the reference?"

"He will. Maybe not straight away, but he will google it."

"And he's paying for this?"

He grinned then. "That's the best part."

"Are we having them delivered? Or did you want to deliver them yourself?"

He hummed as he considered this. "I think I should like to deliver them myself."

"They'll be heavy. I can have one of the guys help you carry them if you want." The Vintage Emporium was only up the block. "Or maybe I could even help you deliver them, just to see his face."

He brightened at that. "It would be only fair that you do."

"They'll take a short while to be prepared," I said. "Did you want to come back?"

"I might duck next door and grab a coffee." He waved his ex's credit card. "Want one?"

I laughed again. "No, I couldn't. But thanks."

"Okay, I'll be back," he said, disappearing out the door.

"Lina," I called, and she came straight out. I explained the two bouquets we wanted and the budget, and we got straight to work. We couldn't always accommodate rush orders but this one was unusual. And fun. And he was cute, so . . .

When I'd thought earlier that today was going to be a great day, I didn't have this in mind. It wasn't every day we got orders for revenge arrangements.

"Uh, these are some bold choices," Lina mused.

"And it's exactly what you think it means," I said with a laugh. "His boyfriend cheated on him."

She laughed as she fixed the black basil leaves. "Well, that would explain these."

I had most of the larger arrangement done by the time he came back in, large iced coffee in his hand. He slid his expensive sunglasses up onto the top of his head. "Oh, these are looking perfect," he said.

I left mine in Lina's very capable hands.

I nodded to the customer, whose name I still didn't even know. "Come over to the desk and we'll sort out the paperwork." I took the iPad and opened the order form. "Customer name. Am I writing in his name or yours?"

"His, probably," he said flatly. "He is paying, and let's be real, all insults should probably be tax deductible."

I snorted. "True."

"I'll give him that much."

"Generous."

"Better than what he probably gave me," he mumbled.

My gaze shot to his. "Oh, uh. Yeah. Sorry about that."

He waved me off. "I've been to the clinic. I'm fine, but still . . . if I weren't, we'd be finding a way to get me the murder flowers."

I laughed again. God, I hadn't laughed this much in a long time.

I pulled up the Vintage Emporium customer details and copied it over, wondering how on earth I could ask this guy his name without encroaching on privacy issues.

"Keats," he said.

My head shot up at my name. He was reading the framed certificates on the wall, then my name tag on my apron. "So, Keats McCulloch. Is that your real name?"

"Ah . . . yes?"

"You don't sound sure."

"Well, I'm sure it is. Just not sure why you'd think it wasn't real."

"It's unusual."

"I have my father to thank for it," I volunteered.

"A fan of the literary arts?"

"Yes."

"It's a fabulous name. Right alongside Lord Byron and Percy Shelley, and here I am sounding like an old person's home."

I tried not to laugh and failed. "An old person's home? Like Shady Pines?"

"Linden Acres."

I swallowed the outburst of laughter that almost escaped. "Oh."

"Thank you for not laughing. I can see the restraint it cost you. I also appreciate the *Golden Girls* reference."

I laughed so hard I snorted. Even Lina cast me a look over her shoulder. "Linden Acres. It's a nice name."

"Nice." He nodded. "In my industry, having nice used as a descriptor is a kiss of death."

"And what is your industry?"

I couldn't be blamed for asking when he was the one who brought it up.

"I'm a personal shopper."

"Oh." I don't know why that surprised me. I had no idea that was a real job. "What exactly does a personal shopper do?"

"I work for people who have more money than time, basically. They give me lists of what they need for an upcoming event or vacation, and I make sure they have it."

It certainly explained why he came in here with a list of research.

"That sounds fascinating, actually. Bet you've seen some crazy things."

His eyes went wide. "So many things," he said with a nod. "All of which my NDAs prohibit me from telling you."

I chuckled. "I am absolutely not surprised by that. But it does explain why you have such impeccable taste."

He gave me a cute little nose-scrunch smile. "Thank you."

"So, are you also billing your ex for your time today?" I asked.

He seemed confused for a moment. "I wasn't. Why do you ask?"

"Just wondering how long you wanted this order to take. Are you paid per hour or per job?"

His smile was slow spreading. "I do like the way you think, Keats McCulloch. Maybe I should send him a bill."

"Maybe you should." I leaned in closer and whispered, "And send him a bill for any fees the clinic charged you."

He grabbed my arm and inhaled deeply. "I love this. My villain era will be my best yet."

I burst out laughing. Villain era.

This guy was funny. And *really* cute.

Lina brought the first finished bouquet to the counter where we were. It was the largest of the two and she'd added greenery and a black ribbon. It was truly striking, despite the message it gave.

"Oh, this is perfect," Linden said wistfully. "It's almost a shame to waste them on him."

He paid, and I handed him my business card. "If you ever need to tell someone else they're dead to you, just give me a call."

It wasn't lost on me that I was giving him a card with my mobile phone number on it, and when his eyes shot up to mine, maybe it wasn't lost on him either. "You know, I just might," he replied.

Lina cleared her throat. "Robbie's busy. You'll need to deliver these yourself," she said to me, then went to the door and held it open. Her cheeky smirk told me she knew exactly what she was doing.

So, armed with one bouquet each, we headed towards the salon.

"Are you sure you want to deliver this with me?" he asked. "I didn't think the boss did deliveries."

"Absolutely. I want to see his face. And I don't expect my staff to do anything I wouldn't do."

He smiled at that. "I like you, Keats McCulloch."

When we got to the salon, he took a deep breath and pushed the door in with his butt, giving me a winning smile as he did. "Here goes nothing."

I followed him in. The salon itself was very upmarket and fancy, with marble and black accents. Linden slid the huge bouquet onto the reception desk and the owner, Linden's soon-to-be ex, came out, inspecting the flowers. His expression was curious, a little concerned, maybe even a little put off.

"Green and black is a . . . bold choice," he sniffed. Then the douche looked me up and down with as much distaste as he did the flowers, then back to the bouquet. "I mean, they're beautiful . . . I guess. I'll have to look up what these flowers mean before I decide if I love them."

With a laugh, I handed Linden the other bouquet and clapped his arm. "You deserve so much better," I said, and I walked out into the warm spring sunshine.

Yep. Today was a great day.

CHAPTER TWO
LINDEN ACRES

IT'D BEEN A BUSY TWO WEEKS SINCE THE OFFICIAL break up with Jason. Busy, productive, which was a good thing. I wasn't even sad about it. In fact, I felt a little empowered.

Oh, he'd googled what the flowers meant all right.

Right there in his salon in front of everyone.

The way he'd glanced from his phone to me with a shocked and horrified look on his face was all the glory I'd needed.

"I was going to go with a flower that said *betrayal*, but *I hate you* and *you're dead to me* was so much better," I'd said to him. "Given there's no flower that translates to *you should have kept your dick in your pants*, I went with what's in my heart."

People in the salon had gasped.

One lady had lifted her phone to record us.

I didn't care. I hoped she did.

"Oh, and you can expect a bill for my time today, and one from the sex health clinic because god only knows what diseases your cheating dick gave me."

The clinic had been totally free, but after Keats had mentioned it, I thought it packed a sweet little punch.

Someone had laughed.

Not Jason. *Oh no, he looks like he's about to choke on something.*

I'd stopped at the first chair on my way out. A lady with fresh highlights, dressed head to toe in Prada and YSL. "Darling, that colour is fabulous on you." It was. She looked amazing. I handed her my card. "If you ever need a personal shopper, you give me a call."

And then I'd walked out.

Happy and empowered.

I'd waited for the crash to come, but it never did. I'd waited for the bitterness that usually followed to come, but it never did.

I also waited for the apology from Jason to come—only so I could tell him to fuck all the way off—but that never came either. Not that I was surprised.

So yes, I'd wasted three months of my life with that cheating jerk and I was happy to be rid of the garbage from my life.

I could focus on my work and on myself. And my friends, of course. Who all told me they never liked Jason from the very beginning and I should have listened . . .

Hindsight was always crystal clear.

And I fully intended to focus on myself for the foreseeable future. No more men, no more dating, no more fast-acting, smooth-talking jerks. I wasn't even looking for hook-ups. No more casual meetings, no more Grindr.

"Oh, come on," Cory tried. "It'll be fun, and you can forget about what's-his-name."

Cory was my best friend and I loved him with my whole

heart. I should have listened when he'd warned me about Jason, but I hadn't. Not a mistake I'd make twice.

"I've already forgotten about him," I replied. "And like I said, if and when I'm ready to start looking again, I'll need your stamp of approval before there's a second look."

"Promise me this time," he said, clinking his glass to mine.

"I promise." I nodded to the dance floor. "Now go swish your sexy little arse for the boys."

He brightened, downed his cocktail, and slinked his way to the dance floor. He was such a little slut and I adored him. Over-the-top, fem, loud and flamboyant, fierce and loyal, and the kindest soul I'd ever met.

I could joke with him about the prospect of meeting someone new, even though I was adamant that day would be years from now. I was so done with this scene: sitting in a bar, watching the men as they danced, as they eyed each other, sized each other up. Some looking for forever. Some looking for a quick fuck.

I wanted nothing to do with any of it.

Happy to chaperone Cory until he found someone else to leave with. But for me?

No.

Yet a certain someone's business card kept burning a hole in my wallet.

I knew it was in there. I could feel it like an invisible burr. A splinter, even.

The man with the perfect name and the kind eyes. The man who stopped time with every burst of laughter. The man who touched my arm, looked me right in the eye and told me I deserved better.

Keats McCulloch.

What kind of ridiculously fancy pants name was that?

I had his card, his number, and I knew where he worked.

What I didn't know was if he was in any way inclined to dick me—not that I was looking—and what I also didn't know was why I couldn't get him out of my head.

Yes, you do know. You just don't want to admit it.

I threw back my vodka and lime, not for any other reason than to shut my inner monologue up.

Eye contact.

He'd held eye contact like a heat-seeking missile, locked and loaded, like he had absolutely nothing to hide.

Any man in this bar couldn't hold eye contact for two seconds without looking away, looking for someone else, looking for an excuse to bail.

Jason could never hold eye contact, not even for a second, and now I knew why.

He was always hiding something and afraid I'd see the truth.

Keats Perfect-Name McCulloch never looked away once. In fact, it was me who had to look away. I felt scrutinised . . .

No, I felt seen.

Seeing Cory was now firmly latched on to some huge Arab guy—his very favourite kind—I knew he was five minutes away from leaving, so I beat him to it. I weaved my way through the crowd, only having to peel two slimy hands from my arse along the way, and came up behind Cory.

His dancing partner seemed to think his luck had changed for the better when I put my hands on Cory's hips. "I'm going home," I yelled over the music. "Be good, and call me tomorrow."

He let his head drop back onto my shoulder and laughed, grinding his dick against Mr Huge's crotch.

"Wanna join us?" the guy asked. "I can service both of you."

Service.

Once upon a time, I'd have found that funny, maybe even considered his offer.

But not anymore.

"No thanks," I said. "Service him twice instead."

Cory laughed. "Love you, Linden."

I smacked his arse, making him groan like the little slut he was, and I left him to it. The night was still young. It was a warm spring night. Happy people filled the streets, and normally I'd have kicked on. Maybe found an alfresco restaurant on the waterfront.

But all I wanted to do tonight was to go home.

I wanted to have a hot shower and scrub the nightclub off me, maybe watch some TV, or just go straight to bed.

It wasn't like me.

Well, it wasn't like the *old* me, but the been-cheated-on me wasn't interested in any of this shit anymore. I just wanted to go home.

It was a quick Uber to Newtown, and twenty minutes later, I was on the couch in my small one-bedroom unit, showered and wearing my comfy trackies and an old T-shirt, watching a re-run of *House and Garden*, and eating leftover tteokbokki.

Then something horrifying occurred to me.

Oh, dear god.

I snatched up my phone and sent a message to Cory.

I know you won't get this until after your servicing from the Arabian stallion and I truly do hope you can walk tomorrow but you should be the first to know that I'm one step away from being your Aunty Cath

You know I love her but I'm a hot twenty-
six-year-old gay man, not a middle-aged
lesbian

I'M WEARING SWEATPANTS WATCHING
HOME RENOVATIONS ON TV WHILE
EATING KOREAN FOOD HELP ME

Just kidding. Enjoy your thorough dicking

But we need to talk about this tomorrow

All my messages were left unread, which was hardly surprising, considering he was probably getting railed with a ten-inch dick right about now.

So I sent him one last message.

Wasn't kidding about being able to walk
tomorrow. If you need anything like ice
packs, local anaesthetic, call me

Then I finished my tteokbokki while watching some dude on TV rip out old decking, replace it, prime it, then oil it, and for a brief second, I considered texting Cory's Aunty Cath to discuss. Before I could hate myself even more, I turned the TV off and put myself to bed.

Before midnight on a Saturday night.

Such a rockstar.

I WAS IN FOR ANOTHER BUSY WEEK.

I had a client appointment on Monday morning and a

new-client appointment in the afternoon, plus a request for a staging on Tuesday. I didn't do those often, thankfully. They were time consuming and stressful, which was why they paid well. Stagings for real estate listings could take two whole days, so I was booked up until one appointment on Friday morning.

But my Monday morning client was a regular and I adored her.

Armed with her favourite coffee, I was at her home just after nine o'clock. She opened her door and saw what I was holding. "Oh, you are a darling," she said, giving me a kiss on the cheek.

"And you're hosting the party of the year in seven days," I said. "We better get you organised."

And that's what I did.

I organised people for all kinds of occasions. Sometimes it was clothes, jewellery, or perfume. Sometimes it was an entire wardrobe. Sometimes it was home décor. Sometimes it was urgent because they'd just found out they were on the redeye to New York. And sometimes purely because a client was short on time and needed something for no other reason than they wanted it.

My clients were all typically very wealthy. They appreciated my eye for detail, and the fact I knew every trend, every market, every hottest fashion. Some didn't care about price tags; some wanted exclusive sales. Some wanted every minor detail organised; some wanted me to run with my own ideas.

The fact I could message a client and be like, *So, I'm in Saint Laurent right now and those jeans you couldn't get in London they now have in stock, in your size. Yes or no?* was a testament to their trust in me.

I had a memory for detail and a knack for being as much or as little as they needed me to be.

Monday's client was organised to a point where she had a list of necessities for her anniversary party but left the details up to me. She was hosting, so besides the usual outfit requirements, she was running low on her favourite YSL lip colour, and she also wanted a small gift for each of the forty guests coming.

Oh, and a watch for her husband.

Could I do all of this in five days? Even with everything else I had going on?

Easy.

Monday afternoon's client was new. He was travelling to Singapore and Tokyo for work and play, and with deadlines approaching and zero time to spare, one of his friends was a client of mine and had sworn to him he needed me.

He really did.

Need me, that is.

In one minute, I'd told him what the weather was going to be like in both destinations, which would determine his styling choices, and given he had meetings and both work and casual parties to attend, I ran through a list of wardrobe and travel essentials.

New luggage, new wardrobe, gifts for work associates, and a new skin care routine . . . because he needed that too.

All in a day's work.

Tuesday's appointment was with Megan Morano Properties. I would often do staging for them for photoshoots or open listings. Nothing major and certainly no full furnishing jobs, but personal touches and tailored marketing were more my forte.

This particular job was for an exclusive residential suite with a very particular target demographic. Of course, they needed it for a personal viewing on Friday.

Megan handed me the client list of those viewing the property. "Can you handle it?"

I knew exactly what I had to do, and that little business card that had been burning a hole in my wallet for weeks burned a little hotter.

"Of course I can," I said, confident and reassuring.

And with a belly full of butterflies, I found myself walking into Bloom, hoping like crazy that a certain florist with his perfect name was working.

That he was single and that he slotted somewhere toward the queer end of the Kinsey Scale.

"Good afternoon!" The lady behind the counter smiled brightly as I opened the door. She was the same woman who had helped Keats the other day and *not* the person I wanted to see. Her name tag declared her to be Lina.

I tried not to show my disappointment. "Hi," I said, walking up to the counter. "I was in a few weeks ago with a fairly specific order. The guy who helped me was great. I was hoping he might be in today."

She stared at me for half a second and I could see it in her eyes when the penny dropped. "Oh, the breakup flowers!"

I chuckled. "That's one way to put it. But yes, that's me."

She smiled. "So, did the flowers work?"

I nodded. "Message was received and understood, yes."

"Good, good," she said with a nod. "So, oh, the man who helped you . . ."

"Keats."

She seemed surprised that I remembered his name. "Yes, Keats."

"Not a name one forgets," I added.

"No," she murmured, but there was the beginning of a smirk there too. "He's out the back. I'll just grab him for you."

Oh. He was here.

My stomach was suddenly full of butterflies, which was ridiculous. My heart was a little jittery too.

What the hell?

Then the staff-only door swung inwards, and he appeared. Tall and as handsome as I remembered. His blue eyes were bright, and his smile was wide, and my heart jittered a little harder.

Christ, get a grip.

"Hey," he said, wiping his hands on his apron. "You're back. Lina said you had a specific request. Need another bouquet of murder flowers?"

I laughed. "Ah, no. A rather specific request, yes. No murder flowers this time."

He grinned at me. "Good. Glad to hear that."

I stood there smiling at him, him smiling back at me, and now my heart was feeling a little constricted. I had to make myself look away. I nodded to the door he'd come through. "If you were busy . . . I didn't mean to interrupt."

"You're not interrupting," Lina said quickly. She half shoved Keats towards me. "I'll go finish that order you were working on."

He tried to argue but she was already gone.

"Is she trying to get rid of you?" I joked. It was definitely suss, but the blush on his cheeks told me it was something else. Something else that made the butterflies in my belly swoop.

"Ahhh," he said, swallowing hard and wiping his hands on his apron again. "No, she's just . . . she's just . . . She was saying you have a specific request today?"

Right. Straight to work.

But the flirting was so much fun, I just couldn't help myself. I fingered a pretty flower in the stand next to me. "Yes. I'm doing a staging for a real estate suite with a very tailored client list, and I thought of you."

His eyes met mine. "Oh?"

"Yes, you were very helpful with my last request."

"Oh."

That was definitely a flicker of disappointment. I saw it before he schooled it away.

The thrill made me smile. "And it was a good excuse to see you again."

His eyes widened this time. "Oh, uh . . ."

I'd forgotten how fun the flirting game could be. I bit my bottom lip, like the little hussy I apparently was. "Yes, you really helped me out last time and you gave me your card. I was going to call and say thank you, but then the work thing came up and it was a good excuse to see you instead."

He fought a smile as he nodded, studying the flower I was still touching. "Right. And your . . . ex. He got the meaning of the flowers?"

"Oh, yes. He also got a bill for my time and from the clinic. Thank you for suggesting that, by the way."

He laughed, then his eyes met mine again as he nodded. "So your villain era is going well."

I snorted. "Well, it was short-lived. I'm in my middle-aged-lesbian, home-renovation era now."

He laughed, surprised. "Oh, that's . . . quite the leap."

"Well, my best friend seems to think it will pass," I said with a sigh. "That my desire to stay in and avoid men at all costs is just a passing phase, but honestly, I'm not sure. My days of clubbing and hangovers can stay behind me for all I care. He, on the other hand, is still in his whore era." I blinked at him. "Him, my best friend, not me. My god, the things that boy tells me makes me blush, and I'm no prude."

Keats chuckled. "Right. Well, as long as he's happy."

"Oh, he is, believe me. Especially if it involves a top of centaur proportions, if you know what I mean." I sighed.

"Well, this conversation went in a direction I was trying to avoid. Do you have any flowers that can wipe the last few minutes from someone's memory? That you could inhale deeply perhaps? Then we can act like this whole conversation didn't happen."

He laughed again, and he was now standing closer . . . *Was he this close before?*

"Wow, you're a lot closer than I remember, and your eyes are bluer than I remember. Did you use the memory-wiping flower on me?"

God, shut up, Linden. Just stop talking.

He pressed his lips together to stop from smiling, his cheeks a pretty pink. "Uh, no. There's no such flower, I believe."

"That's probably a good thing," I murmured. "Not that you'd let me have them, like you didn't let me have the murder flowers."

"Probably just as well," he said. "I don't think you're built for prison."

I snorted. "Pretty sure they'd love me in prison."

He laughed again, such a deep, warm sound. "There's nothing wrong with staying in, you know," he mused. "Clubbing is overrated, and hangovers are the worst."

"So you stay in too?" I asked.

"I do."

"Do you watch home renovation shows?"

"I've seen some."

"They have a cooking and a gardening segment," I added. "Kinda great all-round entertainment for middle-aged gays, if I'm honest."

He put his hand to his chest. "Well, I'm only thirty. Not sure that constitutes middle-aged."

Hmm. Four years older than me.

But he didn't discredit the gays part of that comment, so . . .

"I think middle-aged is more a state of mind," I went on. "I'm only twenty-six, yet I've lived through my hussy era, my villain era, so that really only leaves the middle-aged era."

He chuckled. "Is that the lifespan of the modern gay man these days?"

I sighed. "Apparently. My villain era was far too short. I should reconsider moving on so fast."

"Maybe you moved on so fast because you weren't as into him as you might have thought."

I met his eyes, not sure what to make of that.

He smiled at me. "But I think all villain eras should be short-lived or one might veer into a bitter-gay era or a spiral era, and those can't be fun. Maybe you should change course; see where the grass is greener type of thing."

Was he . . . was he flirting with me?

"The grass is greener where it's watered," I murmured.

"True. Where it's watered by everyone in the relationship. If only one person is watering the grass, it'll never be green enough."

I smirked at him. "Sounds like you know a thing or two about that."

"Hm. Maybe. It was probably one of those home renovation shows with gardening tips I watched in my suddenly single era."

I laughed. "Right. And how's that era working out for you now?"

"Well, it's been fun, but it's been a long era, so it'd be nice to come out of it sometime."

Well, damn.

He was flirting, right? That's what this was?

I let out a breath, entirely unsure how to ask outright. I

looked around his showroom, full of flowers, searching for some way to broach this . . . "So, if you were looking at maybe leaving the single era behind and maybe enter your dating era again, which kind of flowers would you choose? A white gardenia for feminine attraction, or pink carnations for a woman's love, or—"

"I'm more of a green carnations kind of guy," he said.

Green carnations were for homosexuality.

Right. Well, that answered that.

"That's . . . that's good to know," I said, trying to play it cool and failing terribly. "It just so happens that I'm also a green carnations kind of guy. Which is terribly convenient, don't you think?"

He was trying not to smile too big. "I think it might be."

"So, is there a flower that means *we should totally meet for coffee?*"

His eyes met mine, his cheeks a lovely blush. "Not sure there is."

"What about a flower that says *dinner sometime?*"

He drew his bottom lip in between his teeth, still fighting a smile. "I think chickweed means *we should meet again,* but it's not specific to coffee or dinner."

I looked around his shop. "Do you have any chickweed?"

"No," he said. "But I do have a phone number. Which I believe you already have."

"I do. And there's another coincidence, because so do I. Have a phone number, that is. I should totally give it to you." I shrugged. "In lieu of chickweed, that is."

"Oh, of course. In lieu of chickweed. A fair exchange."

And then we stood there just smiling at each other again until Lina came through the door, holding a rather large arrangement of flowers. It seemed to spur Keats into work-mode. "Right. The flowers you wanted. We should probably do that."

"We probably should," I said, ignoring the way Lina was trying not to watch us. "So what are the chances of getting one of these by Friday?" I showed him a picture on my phone. "In an ornate pot, and it needs to be bearing fruit."

"Oh, wow. You really do have obscure requests."

I chuckled, enjoying the moment of him standing close enough to look at my phone screen. He smelled so good . . .

"That's a kumquat," he said. "I would need to make some phone calls, but it's not impossible."

"Awesome. And I'll also need two arrangements: one of red orchids, definitely no white, and the other arrangement of apple and magnolia blossoms. I was thinking for a table display."

"Okaaay," he said slowly. "I'm going to assume there's a cultural significance."

"You would assume correctly." I sighed. "My client is showing an exclusive residential suite to some Chinese business partners. To anyone else, these flowers and the kumquat plant will just be pretty. But these people will get the significance. They mean prosperity, success, and wealth, and are like a token of goodwill."

"You like flowers with meaning, huh?"

I thought about that for a second. "It seems I do. Though to be honest, I didn't until my awful ex got into the whole floriography thing, as if he was some knowledgeable guru." I rolled my eyes. "He's probably into reading tea leaves this week, so whatever. And the cultural significance thing and knowing which items speak to which person is more an art of gift giving and knowing your client and what they need, which is my area of expertise. It's what I do."

"I'm impressed," he said quietly.

It made my heart knock against my ribs.

"So can you do it for me?" I asked. When his wide eyes met mine, I realised how that sounded. "The flowers and the kumquat tree, I mean."

"It should be fine," he said, amused. "I'll make some calls about the tree and let you know. Though I'll need your number for that."

"Smooth," I said, taking his business card from my wallet for his number, and I sent him a text.

Hey

He took his phone from his apron pocket, read the message, and met my gaze. "Hey."

I blushed.

I freaking blushed.

"I should change your name in my contacts," he said, thumbing his screen. "So I don't accidentally ask one of my suppliers out for dinner."

The butterflies in my belly swooped and somersaulted. "Yes, that'd be a shame."

He spoke slowly as he typed. "Lin. Den. A-cres."

"You remembered?"

He smiled, still looking at his screen. "Hard to forget a name for an old people's home."

I resisted the urge to shove him. "Oh, okay, Mr perfect-name Keats McCulloch."

He grinned spectacularly. "Did you know, floriographically speaking, Linden means *love in marriage*?"

Oh my god.

"Well, no. I did not know that. But maybe we should start with coffee or dinner first."

He laughed. "Sound plan."

"So," I hedged. "Is that something you knew already? Or did you look that up after I left last time?"

"I might have looked it up."

So he'd thought about me? Probably not as much as I'd thought about him, but still.

More customers came in, and Lina was already busy. Another guy came out through the staff door to serve them, but it wasn't fair of me to take up so much of his time. "You're at work, I should let you go," I offered.

"Okay," he said. "I'll make some calls about the tree and see what I can arrange before I create the job file for you. I have your number, so . . ."

"So you should use it."

His eyes met mine and he smiled. "I will."

"Okay, then," I said, stepping toward the door. "I have a thousand things I need to do."

"Wait," he said, going to a bunch of flowers at the far wall. He plucked out one single flower. "For you."

Oh. My heart was back to thumps and jitters.

The flower was red and orange, looked like a poppy, but different. "Oh. Is this some kind of poppy? Is that for remembrance? Or are you suggesting I put you to sleep like Dorothy in the *Wizard of Oz*? Am I that boring?"

He laughed. "No, it's an Austrian rose."

"Oh."

He cleared his throat and shoved his hands in the pocket of his apron. "Uh, maybe search the meaning when you leave?" His eyes darted to Lina who was with some customers pretending she wasn't listening to us.

"Okay," I said, feeling giddy and ridiculously excited. I took the flower and with a smile, not wanting to leave but needing to, I took a step back. "Call me. Or I will text you about the . . . chickweed."

He laughed. "See that you do."

With my heart thumping, I managed to leave his store and pulled out my phone, googling the meaning of Austrian rose.

Thou art all that is lovely.

I stopped walking because my knees went weak, and I had to take a second to breathe.

I looked back at his store, wondering if he was watching me. Hoping he was. I laughed, so unreasonably excited, before continuing on my way. With my phone still in my hand, I called Cory.

He answered on the second ring, but I didn't give him a chance to speak.

"Oh. My. God. Cory, you will never guess what just happened."

CHAPTER THREE
KEATS

WE GOT THROUGH THE RUSH OF CUSTOMERS, AND IT wasn't until mid-afternoon that we had a moment to stop and breathe. I'd made some phone calls about the kumquat tree and sent Linden a text.

> Good news about the tree. Price is a bit ridiculous. Call me to discuss when you have a moment.

I left it at that, ignoring the thrill it gave me.

"I told you he'd be back," Lina said with a knowing smile.

"Yes, well," I tried. "We'll see."

She had said he'd be back after the first time he'd come in. She'd said she hadn't heard me laugh like that in a long time and how nice it was. She'd also sworn that he was very cute, and he was looking at me a certain way.

I'd argued that he was in the middle of a breakup and how we shouldn't read into anything that simply wasn't there. Ignoring the fact I'd given him my card and how he hadn't called me.

But then he *had* come back in, and there was definite flirting. Also the definite exchange of numbers and the suggestion of a coffee or dinner date. He'd hedged around the subject of interest, asking if my flower of choice would be for a woman.

I'd told him I was more of a green carnations kind of guy.

I'd never said anything so ridiculous in my life.

But the way he'd smiled after I'd said that?

Totally worth it.

So I texted him about the tree. Technically a work text but still, it was now an open channel of communication. The ball was in his court.

"If he texts back or if he calls," I added, trying to compartmentalise and over analyse every little thing.

"If he texts, it means he's busy. Most people prefer to text these days. You know that."

"Yes, but if he was really interested—"

My phone rang on the counter, Linden's name on the screen.

Lina laughed. "If he were interested, he'd call?"

I scowled at her and picked up the phone, answering. "Linden," I said.

"The one and only," he replied. "Literally. Surely there isn't anyone else out there with the name of an old people's home."

I laughed before trying not to smile, giving a too-happy Lina a stop-it glare as I took the call into the backroom.

"So, the kumquat tree," he said. "You found one?"

"I did. The price is steep though."

"This client will pay," he said simply. "No questions. She'll then use it as a thank you gift for the buyers when they settle the contracts."

"Oh, okay. And the two bouquets," I went on.

"Also fine. Just send me the invoice. I'll also need delivery. I can send you the address. It's in Millers Point, so not far."

Millers Point? A very expensive address. "Nice."

"Very."

"So, coffee," I said, then winced because, god, what the hell was I doing?

He hummed. "I do like coffee."

It sounded as if he was smiling. "I was hoping you did, because if I were to ask if you wanted to meet me for one sometime, it'd be awkward if you didn't like it."

He chuckled. "And we couldn't have it being awkward now, could we?"

"I don't know. I think I'm managing it."

He laughed this time. "This isn't awkward. I googled the meaning of the Austrian copper rose, so there can't be any awkwardness. On a scale of one to ten, you're already at an eleven so . . ."

"Eleven? Great. So no pressure to maintain that level of non-awkwardness then."

"No pressure at all."

I stood there smiling like an idiot for a few long seconds.

Speak, Keats. Say something . . .

"So, coffee," I managed. "Is Saturday or Sunday okay for you?" Then I felt the need to explain. "I work at the shop during the week, that's all. Though I could probably take a short break around two o'clock most weekdays, if that suits? Or dinner, any night. Though fair warning, I don't do late nights because I'm up pretty early every day to hit the markets."

God, now stop speaking, Keats.

"Sorry," I tacked on. "That was a lot."

He laughed. "I don't do late nights anymore either. I'm in my middle-aged-lesbian era, remember? If you want to order Korean takeaway and watch reruns of *Home and Garden* or *Love It Or List It*, I'm your guy. It's my life now."

"Is it bad if I said that actually sounds like my kind of night?"

He snorted out a laugh. "Awesome. And if we want to live dangerously, we could watch *Home Renovations Gone Wrong*. Or *Million Dollar Designs* and start a new trend for the gays everywhere. *Drag Race* is out. Home-reno shows with men wearing cute tool belts and work boots is in."

"You should organise a float for Mardi Gras."

He gasped. "Do not tempt me."

I laughed. I don't think I'd stopped smiling yet. But it wasn't lost on me that he hadn't agreed to a day or time. "Well, text me when you're free and I'll—"

"Saturday works for me," he said quickly. "Two o'clock. There's a cute coffee place on the King Street Wharf."

My heart hammered against my ribs.

"Okay, great."

"Will I see you on Friday though?" he asked. "Will you be delivering the kumquat tree and bouquets, or will someone else?"

Oh.

"Will *you* be there to oversee this delivery?" I asked.

"Yes, I will be."

"Then I should deliver them myself. You know, to ensure everything is to your liking."

"I do like a man who delivers."

I blushed, thankful he couldn't see me, and it took me a second before I could speak. "Send me through the delivery address and who I need to invoice. And what time you need them delivered."

"I will."

"Okay then. I'm going to hang up now before I make this more awkward for real."

"Okay," he replied. "I'll be in touch."

I hit the End Call button and stood there, leaning against the wall with a stupid smile on my face. I didn't know Lina and Robbie were watching me until Lina spoke.

"So that went well," she said.

Robbie was smiling and he waggled his eyebrows. "The Austrian rose worked, huh?"

I wanted to tell them both to shut up, but I was too busy trying not to smile and laugh. "It might have done," I admitted. "Now I need to find a different flower to give him on our date."

Lina made a high-pitched sound and did a little jumpy dance. "Date?"

"Lime blossom," Robbie said.

"What does that mean?" They knew about this floriography thing with Linden. I mean, we all had a good understanding of the meaning of flowers, but we weren't up to speed on the Victorian ones Linden had referred to.

"Fornication. Well, it kinda means you want to get vulgar with him. There isn't really an olden day Victorian one for *I want to dick you down* but it's a broad meaning—"

I put my hand up. "Uh, no. But thanks. I . . . I don't think that's the message I want to give."

He gave me the kind of side-eye only another gay man could. "I saw how he was looking at you. That boy wouldn't mind getting vulgar, if you know what I'm saying."

I laughed. "Yeah, thanks."

Lina gripped my arm. "A date though. I'm so excited for you. What are you going to wear? Where are you taking him?"

I tried to get my head around any of what had happened today. "Uh, he mentioned a coffee place on the wharf," I said with a shrug. "It'll just be casual, I guess. God, I don't know. It's been . . ." I tried to remember. "A really long time since I've been on a date."

She looked at my hair from several different angles. "Well, a haircut might help. And a new shirt. Something that all the cool kids are wearing these days."

I loved Lina. She'd been my very first employee and had been with me every step of the way of growing my business. She was really like a second mum to me, so her telling me to get a haircut was probably par for the course. But I wasn't sure about the shirt idea . . .

I looked down at myself. "I don't think I need a new shirt—"

"Yes you do," Robbie said a little too quickly. "How many shirts do you own that aren't a work uniform?"

I did a mental flip through my wardrobe.

"That you bought in the last three years?" he added.

"Oh, well . . ."

"Exactly." Robbie sighed. "I'll take you. When is this date?"

"Saturday."

"Plenty of time."

Lina smiled up at me. "Now, about that haircut."

It seemed there was no getting out of this.

"Well, the hair salon on the next block is out of the question," I said flatly. "Maybe I could go to one of those walk-in places."

Robbie let out a horrified gasp. "Dear god, man, no." He took his phone out, scrolled for five seconds, pursed his lips, and put his phone to his ear. "Hello, Charlotte, darling. This is Robbie. I have an emergency haircut for you . . ." He scrutinised me for half a second. "And an eyebrow overhaul . . . Yes, Thursday night?" He looked at me as if he was asking but he didn't even give me time to object. "Perfect. We'll see you then. Yes, love you too."

He pocketed his phone. "Done. Thursday night, seven

o'clock. We'll get you an outfit on the way. And there's a little hole-in-the-wall dumpling place next door. You can buy me dinner."

Okay then.

Lina looked between us and beamed. "This is so much fun."

"You know," I said, trying to recoup some dignity. "I'm not that much of a lost cause. I've been on some dates . . ."

They both stared at me, knowing it was a big fat lie, and at least they had the decency not to laugh.

"I've just been busy," I added.

Robbie grimaced and made a weird hand gesture to my body. "Do we need anywhere else waxed—"

"Oh my god!" I said. "We are not discussing that. He either likes me just as I am, or he doesn't like me."

Lina did a fist pump. "Yes!" But then she relented. "Though a little manscaping is never a bad thing."

"Oh my god." This was horrifying. "Can we please never talk about this ever again? Ever. I beg of you. Actually," I said, raising my chin. "As your boss, I forbid it. A new workplace rule. Effective immediately."

Robbie snorted and Lina bounced up on her toes. "You're going on a date! I'm so excited for you."

I sighed.

It was going to be a long few days.

ROBBIE'S IDEA OF GETTING ME AN OUTFIT WAS basically bringing his boyfriend along. Tan was a pocket-sized tornado of a guy, and between the two of them, I was shoved in and out of changerooms with armfuls of clothes until they approved.

It was like *Queer Eye,* only worse. Between Tan appraising me up and down with his finger to his chin and Robbie either giving a nod of approval or a squint of *ew, no,* I was now the new owner of three new complete outfits; and a few hundred dollars poorer.

The haircut wasn't much better.

They forced me into the salon chair where Robbie waved his hand in my general vicinity and told a very amused Charlotte to "Please fix this."

Which she did, I will admit.

She was very good, and lovely, and she clearly adored Robbie and Tan.

I envied Robbie's confidence but also his place in the queer community. He had friends everywhere and he was social, just living his best life. He did things on weekends, he organised group things for fellow gays, and his social calendar was fully booked.

Whereas I went home every night, exhausted. And alone.

Don't get me wrong, I loved my life. I loved my business; it was my passion. I'd worked hard to make it successful. I took that risk all those years ago, and it had paid off.

But there was a social cost.

Seeing the full life Robbie and Tan were living made me want that too.

So if this date with Linden didn't go anywhere, maybe I was ready to put myself back out there.

Maybe it was time.

And when Charlotte removed the cape and asked my reflection if I approved, I gave her a smile and a nod. "Looks great."

I was tidied up, probably as good as I'd ever get, and as ready as I'd ever be.

And I had to admit, it did feel kinda nice.

After buying Robbie and Tan some dumplings as thanks, I took my bags of clothes and went home.

To my small apartment in the city. It was close to my store, close to restaurants and supermarkets, and all I'd needed these last few years.

It was also kinda dull, and there wasn't much of anything that said it was my place.

Maybe it was time I changed that too.

Maybe I should do the whole *Queer Eye* overhaul and get some new décor or furniture. I had the money now, so I could afford it. I'd just never had the inclination.

I told myself it wasn't my date with Linden that was changing my outlook. It was the realisation that yeah, I'd had my head down with my business for so long that it was time to start looking up and around every now and then.

Needless to say, I didn't sleep much on Thursday night.

I knew I'd be seeing Linden on Friday evening when I delivered his order to the address in Millers Point, and I was nervous.

What if the kumquat tree didn't arrive as I'd ordered? What if it wasn't what he'd had in mind? What if it wasn't good enough?

What if *I* wasn't good enough?

On Friday morning, I hit the markets early, like I always did. I went straight to the supplier who had sourced the tree for me . . . and he had it. An ornate fruit-bearing tree as cute as any pictures I'd seen.

For the price Linden was paying for it, it'd want to be.

I took photos of it and, forgetting what time it was, I sent it to him and thumbed out a hasty message.

> One kum quick tree as requested

Then I realised what I'd said. *Oh nooooo.* I began typing like a maniac.

> OMG no

> Please autocorrect why

> Whyyyyy?

> That was supposed to be one kumquat tree, as requested. AS THE PHOTO SUGGESTS idk why autocorrect would do that to me

> I'm sorry

> Please ignore everything

> I'm so embarrassed. JSYK I'll be sending my staff to deliver this because I'm about to walk into the sea

Then I realised I was sending him this barrage of horrifying text messages at 5:36 am.

> OMG I just realised the time. I'm even sorrier now

I had to stop myself from sending him more apologetic messages, because the first ten weren't bad enough. Then I considered tossing my phone into the bin, giving me the excuse that I could then report it as stolen and tell Linden it wasn't me who sent him any messages at all.

That seemed totally fair, right?

I was going to have to cancel my date with him tomorrow. How could I face him now?

I loaded my full order into my van and drove back into the city, to my shop, all kinds of horrified. Lina and Robbie met me at the back door and I was now feeling a little nauseous. "Please be careful with the tree," I said.

"Oooh, look at you with the fancy haircut," Lina said with her usual smile. Then she frowned. "You okay? You look pale."

"I did a bad thing," I said weakly. "I'll be in the cool room."

And that's what I did. I walked into the huge walk-in cool room and sat on a pile of upturned buckets.

Robbie came in and slid a crate onto an empty shelf, then gave me a pitiful look. "What happened?"

I handed him my phone, my spray of messages to Linden still on the screen. "Look at what I did. You might have to scroll up to see the entirety of this disaster."

He scrolled, then stopped. "Oh." Then he laughed. "Oh my."

"I called it a kum quick tree." I stared at him, eyes wide, hands outstretched. "A kum quick tree. Could this get any worse? Yes it can, because then I sent ten more messages, making it so much worse. I can't deliver his order tonight. I can't go on the date tomorrow. I can't—"

My phone beeped in Robbie's hand.

"Oh, he replied," Robbie said, trying not to smile.

"Oh no," I breathed. "What did he say? No, don't tell me. Just toss my phone into the water. I'll tell him it was stolen. I will pretend none of this happened."

He grimaced at me, though it was still a smile. "His reply was hahaha. Actually, Keats, it's three lines of haha in all caps." He turned the phone around to show me.

And there on the screen, was indeed three lines of HAHA-HAHA in all caps.

I deflated. "Awesome."

"He's typing something else," Robbie said. Then he laughed. "He wants to know if that's a magic tree. Does that happen merely on sight? Or does he have to eat the fruit?"

I buried my face in my hands. "This is so bad."

Robbie laughed. "It's perfect. It means he has a sense of humour." Then, because it couldn't possibly get any worse, Robbie took a photo of me and hit Send.

"What? No!" I tried to get the phone from him, but he was too fast, and apparently way faster at texting than me.

He's dying inside

Robbie showed me the screen so I could see. The pic was of me turned to the shelves with my face buried in my hands.

I looked at Robbie. "Why? Why did you do that?"

Then my phone rang, Linden's name on the screen. Robbie grinned and handed me my phone. "That's why. You're welcome, by the way."

I took the stupid phone and hit Answer. "New phone, who this?"

He burst out laughing. "Oh my god, Keats."

"My phone was stolen and it wasn't me," I said.

Linden laughed and laughed. "Oh my god, it was the funniest thing I've ever seen. I'm still not even out of bed yet, and I've never laughed so much."

Oh, great. He's in bed.

I didn't need that visual.

"I'm so sorry," I tried. "Autocorrect sabotaged me."

"I don't know. I rather like the sound of the kum quick

tree. Well, as long as it's not too quick, if you know what I mean."

I sighed. "I'm never going to live this down."

"Who took the photo?"

"Robbie. Who is now fired, by the way. Well, maybe after he delivers your tree because I'm not sure I can face you."

He laughed again. "Yes, you can. Don't feel bad. It was hilarious. And autocorrect gets us all at some point or another."

"Ugh."

"Can I ask you something?"

"Yes. Unless it has anything to do with the name of the tree."

He snorted. "What were you doing with the tree at half-past five in the morning?"

"Oh. The flower markets," I explained. "That's when they open for wholesalers."

"Oh, of course." Then he sighed. "Do you start every day that early?"

"Yep. But you get used to it. It's not so bad. I get to see the sunrise every day, and my day is half over before most people begin theirs."

"Means early nights though."

"Well, yes. Mostly. I don't turn into a pumpkin or anything if I'm out after dark." I frowned, because he was already putting together the incompatible pieces. "I'm usually in bed by nine."

He chuckled. "That's good to know."

"Kinda makes dating hard," I said lamely. "Sorry."

"Did you forget I'm in my middle-aged home-channel-reno-vations-specialty era? If I'm not tucked up in bed watching *House Flippers* or *Bake Off* reruns by eight thirty, I'm a crabby patty."

I laughed at the Sponge Bob reference.

"Please don't feel bad," he said gently. "You totally made my day already. Considering it's not even seven o'clock, that's like a record. And the tree looks perfect. Please say you'll be the one delivering it."

Thank god he couldn't see me smile or blush. "Okay."

"Then I shall see you tonight."

"You shall."

He ended the call, and with a deep breath, I went back out. Robbie took one look at me. "From your smile I can tell *that* went well. You *are* welcome, by the way."

I harrumphed. "Yes, well. I suppose a thank you would be appropriate."

He stood there, waiting, eyebrow raised.

"Thank you," I said with as much dignity as I could muster.

He smiled. "I'm also one hundred percent making his delivery with you because I need to see how this plays out with my own eyes. It's the least you can do."

I considered arguing but I knew that would only make it worse. "Fine. But please don't make it any more awkward."

He barked out an incredulous laugh. "Me? Make it any *more* awkward than a kum quick tree? Believe me, I'll be there to save your arse and salvage any remains from the train wrecks, which you captain solo, my friend."

I sighed, defeated. "Fine."

He took pity on me and handed me the iPad. "Got a busy day," he said. "Probably just as well, so you don't have time to spiral."

I nodded, because that was fair.

He gave me a nudge. "Your hair looks great, by the way. Mr kum quick tree is gonna love it."

I closed my eyes and let out a so-god-help-me breath. "I'll pay you fifty dollars to never say those words to me again."

He laughed. But he didn't take the bet.

I SENT LINDEN A QUICK TEXT TO LET HIM KNOW WE were at the front of the apartment complex and then pressed the doorbell. A few seconds later the doors opened and we could enter the foyer area but couldn't go any further. Then the elevator doors opened and Linden stepped out, smiling, holding a key card.

"Sorry, limited access only. Come on in," he said, holding the doors for us so we could push the trolley in.

There was barely enough room for him, me, and Robbie, plus the trolley with a small tree and two rather large arrangements on it. Not to mention the tension between me and Linden and Robbie trying not to laugh.

"Ah, Linden, this is Robbie," I said, breaking the silence. "Robbie, Linden."

Linden smiled at him. "Oh, the one I have to thank for the photo of Keats when he was dying inside."

Robbie's grin widened. "I am he."

"Oh god," I grumbled.

Robbie gestured to the tree. "And this is . . . ?" He looked at me. "What did you call it?"

I sighed and let my head fall back. "I said you could help me deliver these if you didn't make it more awkward."

Robbie and Linden both laughed, the doors opened, and thankfully we were moving again, pushing the trolley down a very expensive hallway, distracted enough to drop the conversation.

Linden swiped the card and entered a number into the pin pad and held the doors open for us.

The inside of the apartment was the kind of luxury you only saw in movies or magazines. The kind of money that bought this level of excellence was something I couldn't even imagine. And the view . . . Wowzers.

"I've never seen you speechless before," I said to Robbie, who was standing there, mouth open, staring out across Sydney Harbour.

"It's something, isn't it?" Linden said.

Something. That was one way to put it.

He pointed to the main balcony. "I'd like the tree to go there, perfectly centred to the door, if we could, please." He picked up the huge arrangement of apple and magnolia blossoms, which was almost half his height, and placed it on the dining table. "Oh, this is so beautiful. It's perfect."

Robbie and I got the tree positioned right where Linden wanted it, and from inside, the door did frame it perfectly. Whoever was coming to inspect this apartment would have to be impressed.

He was fixing a display of pomegranates and oranges on the kitchen counter. There was also a pile of red cushions on the lounges I assumed he'd brought with him.

"So, when you said you stage apartments," I prompted.

He waved his hand. "I add the personal touches to appeal to the list of buyers."

On a hall stand near the bedrooms stood a rather large sculptured seahorse, red and black, metal, stained glass, and wood. "Is that your touch as well?"

He nodded. "Yes."

"You have very good taste."

He chuckled. "Because this client has a rather large budget, which allows for such things."

Robbie finished perfecting the arrangement of red orchids. "Okay, boss, I'll head out." He made a point of looking at his watch. "It's after five, so if we're done for the day, I'll leave you . . ." He looked pointedly at me and Linden.

I was going to kill him.

"Right. Yes, well," I said. Then I gave Linden an apologetic smile. "I should be going too, if you're busy. I don't want to keep you."

"I'm almost done here," he said. "If you wanted to wait . . ."

"Yes, he does," Robbie said. "Linden, it was so nice to meet you. Have a good date tomorrow. Be gentle with him. He's been out of the dating pool for so long he's forgotten how to swim, if you know what I mean."

I closed my eyes slowly, wishing I could just disappear. "Thanks, Robbie. Awesome. Remind me again why you're still employed?"

He laughed. "Because I'm good at my job." He got to the door, blew me a kiss, and waved to Linden. Then he disappeared into the hall.

I sighed, and when I was finally brave enough to look at Linden, he was grinning. "I like him."

I groaned. "I have mixed feelings about him right now."

Linden laughed. "He seems fun."

"He's pushy, has no filter, and he's feisty." Then I relented. "But he's very good at his job and a close friend of mine, so . . ."

"You told him we have a date tomorrow?"

I grimaced. "Well, yeah, they tortured it out of me. Like waterboarding, without the water or the torture, really. Honestly, I might have just blurted it out because, like he said, it's been a while for me since I dipped my toes into the dating pool."

Linden was still smiling at me. "You had a haircut, I see."

I sighed again, this time defeated. "Robbie and his boyfriend made me. And they made me go clothes shopping." I pointed to my eyebrows. "And this is their doing. Please don't read too much into it. I'm just certain they thought I was heading for priesthood, so they steamrolled me into it. It's honestly better to not argue with them. But I drew the line at manscaping."

His eyes widened.

"I mean, I didn't need it," I added quickly. "Christ almighty, can we just forget today even happened? First with the tree, and then Robbie, and pretty much everything I've said."

He laughed. "I happen to like the kum quick tree."

I laughed, despite the fact it felt like my face was on fire. "Uh yeah, it's been a day."

Linden studied me for a second, a gentle smile pulling at his lips. "I find your nervousness very cute," he said. "And it's refreshing, to be honest."

"Refreshing? Like a cold lemon spritzer on a hot day? Or plummeting into a full body ice bath?"

He grinned at me. "Definitely the spritzer. I just mean that it's nice for a guy to be nervous and excited about a date instead of him being so immune to it that it doesn't matter. I like it."

"Oh, okay." I cleared my throat and shoved my hands into my back pockets and looked around. "So, can I help you here with anything?"

"I just need to fix the cushions," he said.

"Oh, I can do that," I said. Upon closer inspection, I could see each cushion was red silk with gold threads. The kind of detail I'd have never noticed before. I distributed them evenly, but then he came along after me and fixed them, giving each a karate chop on the top to plump them to perfection. I thought I'd done well to even get them on the sofa. "So apparently I can't do that," I added, watching him work his magic.

He chuckled as he perfected everything to within a millimetre. "There's a knack."

I nodded to the pyramid of fruit he'd put on display at the end of the kitchen counter. "And the pomegranates and oranges?"

"A symbol of prosperity and goodwill. And they match the colour scheme."

Jeez.

I was never letting him see the blankness of my place.

"Is your place decorated like this?" I asked. "Where everything has meaning?"

"Like this?" he asked with a laugh. "Uh, no. I lack the budget." Then he gave me a smirk. "Was that you trying to subtly ask to see my place?"

My eyes almost fell out of my head. "What? No! Oh god, I wouldn't . . . I didn't mean . . ."

He laughed and slid his hand onto my arm. "I was joking."

"I was just thinking last night that I needed to do something with my place because I've been so busy these last few years. It's just blank and doesn't say anything about me. Or maybe it says a lot, I don't know. But then I look at what you've done with this place, and you know every little thing about décor, and I can't help but think your place must be amazing, and . . ." I shook my head. "I'm trying to stop talking."

His smile was warm and lovely. "My place is actually a bit messy. I have magazines and binders of style guides everywhere and crates of odds and ends that I might need for work. It doesn't help that my place is small and there's not much room for error."

"Yeah, my place isn't big either," I volunteered. "I moved into the city when I opened my shop. It's close and convenient." I shrugged. "It's all I ever needed these last few years."

"Do you have plants everywhere?" he asked. "I can picture you with plants everywhere."

I snorted. "I have a few. Mostly monstera and kentia. I like greenery. It's peaceful."

He seemed to like that. "I wish I had plants at my place. Maybe you could help me pick some out."

"Maybe I could," I said, my voice soft.

God, he was so good looking. So handsome in his suit pants and button-down shirt. His hair was kinda floppy today, as if he'd run his hand through it a few dozen times.

"Did you need to get back to your shop?" he asked.

I instinctively checked my watch. "No, Lina was closing up today so Robbie and I could make your delivery."

"Great," he said, collecting his messenger bag. "Did you have anywhere you needed to be tonight?"

Oh.

This sounded like it was leading into a question I wasn't prepared for.

"Uh, no. My usual Friday nights include takeout while I go over weekly spreadsheets."

He inhaled sharply. "So you *are* in your middle-aged-gay era too!"

I laughed. "Apparently."

"Well, I know we have our official date tomorrow, so I won't mind if you say no, but I missed lunch today because I've been so busy, so I'm going to grab something to eat at Barangaroo if you wanted to join me?"

"Yes," I answered far too quickly. But then I gestured to my work clothes. "But look at what I'm wearing . . ."

His smile softened. "I don't care what you wear." Then he chuckled. "Though maybe lose the apron."

I pulled at the knot tied at my back and pulled the apron off. "Deal."

I was wearing jeans and a polo shirt and my usual work boots. Absolutely not a date outfit but he genuinely didn't seem to care.

He looked me up and down. "Perfect."

Well, I doubted that, but okay.

"I can drive the van back to my shop and we can walk down," I offered. "It'll be less of a walk from there."

"Sounds good."

He gave the apartment a quick once over, making sure it was all locked and pristine, he took some quick photos, and we left. I felt giddy as we got into my work van, nervous but it also felt good.

It felt right.

There was no awkward silence, no need to fill the gaps in conversation. And after we parked the van and headed toward the wharf area, the evening was perfect. Fading sunlight, warm breeze, people walking past, happy to be finished with work on a Friday.

We found a restaurant that was more of a sports bar, casual and loud. And for an impromptu first date, it was better than a silent fancy restaurant.

We found a table and the waitress came over and handed us menus. "Drinks to start with?"

Linden looked at me and smiled. "Yeah. I'll have a lemon spritzer."

Hm. Refreshing.

I held up two fingers. "Make that two, please." Then I

said, "Can we order food now, if that's okay? He missed lunch."

"Sure thing," the waitress said.

We ordered two quick burgers, and before I could freak out over what to say next, he gave me a shy smile. "Thank you." He rubbed his belly. "I'm starving."

"It's okay. Sometimes they get your drinks, then they get busy, and then it's half an hour before they come back."

He nodded. "I've had a busy day. Had a busy week, actually."

"Good busy? Or horrible busy?"

"Always good busy. I love what I do." His smile lingered, his eyes never leaving mine. "What about you?"

"Always good busy too. I love what I do as well."

"A florist, huh? How did you get into that?"

"My grandmother's garden. Sounds cliché, I know. But it's true. She had roses and gardenias."

"Oh, did you know gardenias need a slightly acidic soil? A pH of about seven. I'm a home and garden expert now."

I laughed. "I did know that, yes."

"Hm. I guess you would."

"When I was in high school, I worked at a florist on Saturdays, and I loved it. Then I actually studied horticulture first, thinking it would suit me, but it wasn't my thing. I lasted six months and changed over."

"It's a lovely job. I mean, who doesn't love to get flowers?"

"Well, your ex probably wasn't a fan."

"Hey, at least they weren't the murder flowers. He should consider himself lucky."

I chuckled. "But it's true. Most flowers are well-received. Funeral flowers are difficult."

He nodded, his eyes fixed on mine. "But you're still

offering a token of beauty in someone's time of darkness, and that's gotta be a good thing."

His eyes. I couldn't look away. I could barely nod. "True. That's a lovely point of view."

The waitress placed our drinks in front of us, finally breaking the eye contact between us.

Oh boy.

My heart was thumping, and I sipped my drink. "So, what about you? How did you get into personal shopping?"

"By accident, really," he said. "I've always been very good at it. I love fashion and shopping. But I started as a personal assistant. I was eighteen and basically organising this person's entire life. When I was twenty-one, they ended up moving to LA, and by then I had contacts, their friends and associates, and they knew to ask me if they needed something sourced. That's how it started."

"It sounds interesting, for sure."

"Beats an office job. I would literally die in a cubicle job. I'm not even kidding. And I get to spend someone else's money, so it's all a win for me."

"What's the hardest part?"

He thought for a second. "Seeing how they live—the houses, cars, travel, the parties—and knowing that income gap between them and me is a bridge I'll never cross. Short of a multimillion-dollar lotto win, or something."

I nodded with a smile. "I can see how that would suck."

"What about you? What's the worst part of being a florist?"

"Nothing really," I allowed. "Supply shortages, that kind of thing, but that's part of any business, I guess. Seeing some-one's face as they get a bouquet of roses for a birthday or anniversary while I'm woefully single, that kinda sucks," I said with a laugh. "Or when you know the person getting the flowers is not their wife or husband. Feel like I'm enabling a side piece, ya know? That sucks."

He scrunched his nose up. "Yeah, I could see why that would suck. Unless the jilted party then comes into your store and requests some murder flowers."

I laughed. "Then it's not so bad."

His eyes lingered on mine before he studied the straw in his drink. "So, the reason you've been out of the dating pool and forgotten how to swim, as your friend Robbie called it," he said, his tone casual. "Is there a heartbreak story there?"

Straight into the big questions then . . .

I laughed and sipped my drink for a second to put my thoughts in order. "Uh, no. I'd been with a guy for almost two years. His name was Nigel. We'd grown a bit stale, and things weren't great, and then I began setting up my own business and my time for him, for our relationship, dwindled down to not enough." I sighed. "He called it off, which I totally understood. And honestly, he did us both a favour. I still see him around occasionally. He's been with his current boyfriend for well over a year now, and he's happy, which is good. He deserves that."

Linden's gaze met mine and he considered me for a bit. "That's a good breakup story, as far as breakups go."

I chuckled. "It is. There were no hard feelings, no nastiness. We just grew apart."

He chewed on his bottom lip. "And now? Why are you looking to date again now?"

I felt my cheeks heat. "It's time. The shop is doing well and I can afford to take my hands off the wheel now. My two full-timers, Lina and Robbie, are great. Either one of them could run it for me for a month if I needed them to. Not that I would," I added quickly. "The thought of not being there for a month gives me hives. I actually love what I do, and I love going to work every day, so it's not a chore at all. But I'm not spending every night poring over figures and data or marketing strategies or anything like that anymore. I have more free time, and—" I said with a shrug. "—there are certain parts of dating or relationships that I miss."

He grinned and leaned in. "Like sex?"

I blushed so hard I could feel my skin burn from my scalp to my toes. I tried to laugh it off. "That's one aspect, I guess. Though just so you know, I haven't exactly been a monk these last few years. I mean, I wouldn't be in the running for any playboy trophies, either."

He laughed. "And what are the other aspects?"

I smiled at him. "Like maybe ordering some takeout, getting all comfy on the couch, and watching *Home and Garden* with him."

His smile was slow and wide. "Are you flirting with me, Keats?"

My face burned again, and I'd never been more grateful for the waitress to bring our food. We ordered some drink refills, and I handed Linden his cutlery.

"Oh my god, thank you. This looks so good," he said, shoving some fries in his mouth. "Please don't look at me for the next few minutes while I inhale this. It's not going to be pretty."

I laughed. "Go ahead and eat. I promise not to look."

He wasn't kidding about inhaling it. He was halfway through his burger by the time I'd had one bite, but it was fantastic. And it gave us a few minutes of comfortable silence while we ate.

He put his half-burger down and opted for some fries. "Sorry, but this is so good."

I laughed as I chewed. "Don't apologise. Honestly, it's a

skill that you can take such huge bites and yet eat so delicately."

His cheeks went red. "You weren't supposed to be watching."

"I'm just kidding." Then to prove a point, I picked up my burger and took a massive bite. "It is good," I said with my mouth full.

He laughed, thank god.

We finished our meals, both of us smiling, watching the TV screens that showed various sporting games—American football, English football, Australian rugby league. Not that I was a huge fan of any of it, but it simply just felt good being out and socialising. The atmosphere in the bar was happy and fun and loud, and it really had been far too long since I'd done anything like this.

Linden's phone rang; it was screen-up and I saw the name Megan. "Oh," he said. "The real estate lady from the apartment we were at. I should take this. Do you mind?"

"Not at all," I said. "Take it."

He slipped out from the table. "I'll be two minutes," he whispered to me. "Don't go anywhere." Then he answered the phone as he walked through the crowd to outside.

Like I'd go anywhere.

I checked my phone to fill in some time but saw it was only work emails or messages that could wait until I got home. There were no messages from friends. Because I'd been so busy with my shop these last few years, my friends didn't bother too much anymore. Not that I blamed them.

So yeah, maybe it was time I put my head up and looked around a bit more.

Well past time, even. Long overdue.

So with not much else to do, I took a clean serviette and began folding it because it was better than sitting there like a loser doing nothing. And when Linden came back in and sat across from me, he was smiling.

"So that was Megan. She's the one selling the apartment," he said, like a quick refresher. "Anyway, she called past the apartment to see if everything was perfect, and she loved your arrangements."

"Oh, that's great," I said. "I'm glad she's happy."

"No, I don't think you understand. She loved them. *Loved,* loved. She wants your card for anything else she may have coming up."

Oh.

"Oh, well, that's even better," I said.

"She loved the kum quick tree."

I snorted. "And there I was thinking we'd moved on from that."

"Don't think I will ever move on from that," he said, sipping his drink with a smirk. "But she said the apple blossoms were fabulous, and she loved what I did too, of course. I told her I'd forward her your details."

"I gave you my card, right?"

"Yes, but that's mine. You gave that to me, so she can't have that." He sniffed, trying not to smile. "I'll have to get another one."

I began to take out my wallet. "I'm pretty sure I have—"

"No," he said quickly. "Then I won't have an excuse to come past your shop to get another one."

I chuckled. He was so damn cute. "Oh. Well, you don't need an excuse. And you have my number. You don't need an excuse to use that either."

He pressed his lips together to stop from smiling, but then he noticed what I'd been doing with the serviette. "Oh my god, did you just make that?"

I picked up the folded serviette, which was now a white

flower, and handed it to him. "If I'd known this would be a date, I'd have brought you the real thing."

He took it, his eyes wide, his mouth open. "Keats, it's . . . it's beautiful and perfect."

"A white carnation means my intentions are pure," I said softly.

His eyes went from the flower to me, and he stared. "I, uh . . . thank you. Keats, this is . . ." He swallowed hard and his gaze went back to the flower. "This is perfect." He really did seem taken aback by it. It was just a silly little flower, but he held it as if it were made of gold. "Is the meaning true?" he asked, still not looking at me. "Your intentions, I mean. I want to think you're genuine. You seem genuine, but like you're almost too good to be true, and I haven't had the best luck with guys, so . . ."

Oh.

Oh boy.

I'd kinda forgotten his ex had cheated on him.

"My intentions are true," I said. "And to be honest, I'm so out of the loop with dating . . . What did Robbie say? I'd been out of the dating pool for so long, I'd forgotten how to swim. He's not wrong. So I don't know about too good to be true. I'm not perfect, but what you see is what you get."

His eyes met mine then, and he smiled. "I like that." Then he sighed. "So many guys are out there trying to be everything they're not, and it's exhausting. I just want honesty. I wouldn't have thought that bar was particularly high, but it is, apparently."

"Honesty should be the bare minimum."

He groaned. "Right? Like the barest. The very least."

I chuckled and watched him as he studied the folded flower I'd given him, twirling it gently. "This just might be the perfect flower. I mean, the kum quick tree was great and all, but this beats it."

I laughed and noticed then that the bar was getting louder and busier. "Should we go?" I checked my watch. "If we leave now, you'll be home in time to watch *Home and Garden*."

He gave me a smile, all warm and lovely, that seeped into my chest. "Yeah."

We paid the tab and fell onto the street, the quiet and cool breeze a welcome reprieve. "It's easy to forget how beautiful this city is," I said. The harbour really was gorgeous and the wharf area—with its lanterns and open restaurants and all the greenery against the water—was really pretty. "I guess I haven't been out in a while. I forgot what it's like down here."

"We were going to come here for our actual date tomorrow," he noted. "Did you still want to? Or you wanna go somewhere else?"

"No, here's fine. Unless you have somewhere else you'd prefer?"

"Here's fine by me too. There's a coffee place further down that I love."

"Perfect."

He stopped walking. "Is everything okay?" I asked.

He pointed to the street up. "I should go this way. I'll Uber it home."

"Oh, sure. Is it far? I can drive you . . ."

He smiled. "No, it's not far." Then he took a deep breath. "I'd like to kiss you. As thanks, for dinner and the perfect flower."

Oh.

"Oh, okay. Um, uh, sure. I'd, I'd like you to do that too," I stammered.

He stepped in, leaned up on his toes, and pressed his soft lips to mine, his eyelids fluttering closed. Just for a moment, one perfect second. Just a soft peck, so innocent, so chaste, but it sent my heart into a frenzy.

He pulled back, his whole face serene. "Thank you, Keats. I'll see you tomorrow."

I'd somehow forgotten how to nod or speak. I think I blinked a few times.

"You okay there?" he asked with a laugh.

I managed a wooden nod, and he stepped back, grinning. "Tomorrow?"

I raised my hand for some reason, and it wasn't until he'd turned and was heading for the street that I found my voice.

"Tomorrow!"

He turned back and laughed, then disappeared out of view. And I stood there for a few seconds trying to remember how to walk. He'd kissed me. And this was how my brain reacted after a quick peck of a kiss? How was I going to react when it was more than a peck? Would there be a deeper kiss?

More than that?

I sure hoped there would be.

God, this was such a thrill, such a rush. I couldn't believe I'd denied myself this for so long. I was so ready for this new chapter of my life.

Now, I just needed to go home and research some Victorian floriography to find the perfect flower to bring him tomorrow.

Maybe while I watched *Home and Garden*.

CHAPTER FOUR
LINDEN

"Hello, darling," Cory said into the phone. "Are you calling me to say you've changed your mind about coming out this weekend?"

"No, sorry. Look, I'm in an Uber on my way home. I just had dinner with Keats—"

"Dinner? Are you eighty? It's not even seven o'clock."

I laughed. "I missed lunch and I was starving."

"Wait, isn't your date with him tomorrow?"

"Yes. This was an impromptu thing. He had to bring flowers to the apartment I did a staging for."

"Oh, yes," he said, only now remembering that I'd told him this. "So he was there and you had a late lunch."

"I'm not sure eating at six o'clock at night could be called a late lunch."

"Okay, sure," he said, sounding a little annoyed. "And how was your . . . dinner?"

I twirled the paper flower between my thumb and forefinger, smiling at it. "Cory, I think I've met the man I'm going to marry."

Silence.

More silence.

"I'm sorry, what? Marry. You want to get married? Since when?"

"Since him. He's perfect. He couldn't be more perfect."

"What did he do to you during dinner? Did he blow you at the table?"

I snorted. "No! That's just it. We talked. And I gave him a sweet little peck on his lips and then we said goodbye. He was just the cutest, and oh my god, Cory." I shook my head. "I don't even know what to say. I can't even describe it. He's just . . ."

"Mr Perfect."

"Yes!"

Cory sighed. "Well, he does have a perfect name."

"I know! He made me a paper flower from the serviette on the table. After all the flower talk we've had, he made me one that can never die."

He made a noise that might have been a gag. "Well, that does sound kinda perfect. So when do I get to meet him?"

I grimaced, grateful he couldn't see. "I'll let you know after tomorrow."

"So you still have the big date with him tomorrow?"

"Yes. It's starting with a coffee."

"And leading to . . ."

"I don't know. I hope so? Is it too soon after Jason? I don't want Keats to think he's a rebound, because he's not."

"When is it too soon to be happy? It's never too soon. You should have never *not* been happy, and the fact you were not happy is Jason's fault, not Keats' fault. So you be happy all you damn want."

I smiled, feeling better about that already. "Thank you."

"And if your date tomorrow goes terrible, just remember I'm going out tomorrow night and you can come with me and we'll find you a tall, dark, and handsome stallion to take your mind off things, okay?"

I laughed. "Okay."

He was quiet for a second. "For what it's worth, I hope it does go well. Even if it means you won't be my wingman anymore and I'll have to slut it up by myself, I hope he's as perfect as you think he is."

This was why he was my best friend. "Thank you. And I'll always be your wingman. As long as I'm home before midnight and sober."

"My god, you are old. You sure you don't want to call my Aunty Cath for tips and pointers on how to live your best middle-aged-lesbian life?"

"I actually wouldn't mind, and if I ever need to go to Bunnings or IKEA, I can take her instead of you."

"Oh, thank god."

I laughed. "Okay, I'm almost home. If you're going out tonight and need me for anything, call me. Otherwise, I'll call you after my date tomorrow."

"I hope you're getting dicked so hard you forget."

I laughed. "This is why I love you."

I ended the call and when I got home, I carefully placed my little perfect paper flower on a saucer and put it pride of place on my bookcase. I took a quick shower, changed into my comfiest trackies and shirt, and planted myself in front of the TV just in time for *Home and Garden* to start.

Perfect end to a perfect day.

Until I got a text message from Keats. It was a photo of his legs in plaid sleep pants outstretched to a coffee table, crossed at the ankles, and his sexy feet. His TV screen showed the opening credits to *Home and Garden*.

I laughed, unprepared for how he'd made a perfect day even perfecter.

I sent him a pic of my view. My legs folded up on the couch; the TV showing the show we were both watching.

A second later, my phone rang.

It was Keats.

"I don't know whether to blame you or thank you," he said, his voice warm and happy. "Does this mean I'm in my middle-aged-gay-man era?"

I laughed. "Possibly. It's not an entirely bad era to be in. I tried to fight it until I realised that I actually really like it. Once you accept it and embrace it, you'll be much happier."

He chuckled. "Oh look, a cooking segment. What is she . . . ? Oh good. Now I want chocolate and raspberry brownies. This will not end well for me. Does this new era include middle-aged-gay-man weight gain?"

"Well, everything's fine in moderation."

"That's also not helping. Now she's eating it fresh out of the oven with ice cream."

"Would you prefer we watch a show on exercise and heart health?"

"I don't think I'm *that* middle-aged," he said with a chuckle. "I'm thirty. I know in gay teen years I'm as good as dead and buried, but my cholesterol is fine."

I laughed. "Next segment is how to select the right indoor plant. Actually, I should take notes because after talking to you, I want to get some greenery for my place. Like a little fern or something."

"A fern?"

"I don't know any other kind of plants. I like the ones that have the droopy vines with heart leaves, but I don't know what they're called."

He chuckled. "There's probably a few, but I think you're talking about a pothos."

"I have no clue. You'd honestly think I should be an expert in these things, considering this is my new favourite show."

"Why were you thinking you needed some greenery?"

"Because you said it was peaceful and I have none at my place, and after I went into your shop and saw how pretty it is with plants and flowers, it got me thinking. And," I added, "truth be told, I'd never spent much time here and a house-plant probably would have died, but these last few weeks I've been at home most nights and on weekends. I've decluttered, sorted my wardrobe, moved some furniture. You know, in my new-me era. I think I should maybe adopt a plant."

"Probably safer than getting a cat," he said. "You know, if you question your mortality rates on a plant."

I laughed. "Fair call."

"I can help you buy a plant tomorrow if you want?" he offered.

"Really?"

"Sure."

I was grinning like a fool. "Okay."

"You know, I was also thinking," he said. "And this is kinda random, so take it for what you will. About my place. It needs some life too. And after Robbie and Tan forced me to go clothes shopping and get a haircut for my new foray into the dating pool, I realised my flat is kinda dull. There's no me here, if that makes sense."

"It makes perfect sense."

"I've just been so busy, ya know?" He sighed. "I've focused so much on my shop, I forgot to focus on me too."

I really liked his honesty. "What do you have in mind? You know I'm a shopping expert, right?"

He laughed. "Yes, but I don't want you to think of me as work."

"I wouldn't."

"Well, maybe I could start small," he said. "And I could get a plant tomorrow too."

"Don't you have plants? I thought you said you did."

He snorted. "Would you believe I have only two?"

"I wouldn't believe that, no."

"It's true."

"Are we going to Bunnings for our second date?" I asked. "And IKEA? Because I would one hundred percent be on board with that."

He chuckled, but before he could answer, the plant I wanted was on the screen.

"Ooh, that plant! That's the one I want."

"Pothos," he said. "They're great."

"Are they easy to keep? Or am I signing its death certificate when I bring it home?"

He laughed. "I'm sure you'll be fine."

I sighed, genuinely perplexed. "So tell me, how does a florist not have a hundred plants in his house?"

"Okay, well, a hundred would be a lot. I have two. Oh, no, three. There's an English ivy in my bathroom. It basically survives on the steam and humidity from the shower. I've had it for years and honestly, I forgot I even had it."

"Poor English ivy."

"She a fighter."

"Maybe I should get myself one of those."

"We can look tomorrow. When we go to Bunnings."

I laughed. "Is it super lame that I'm excited about that?"

"Not at all." It sounded like he was smiling as wide as I was. "Oh, look, they're doing house renovations. Opening the living space by removing a wall. So simple. Until some idiot tries that with a load-bearing wall and the roof caves in. Did you know the success of Bunnings is partly due to shows like this enabling DIY home renovations that then require extensive fixing?"

I laughed. "Well, they get the income from the DIY people, then from the tradespeople who have to fix it. They have the market sewn up."

"True. And I've just realised after saying all that that I'm further into my middle-aged era than I thought. I'm almost at the get-off-my-lawn stage." I laughed and he sighed. "There may be no hope for me. Save yourself while you can."

"We could be the new trendsetters for Fabulous Gays Under Thirty. Instead of sex parties, we can have Bette Midler movie marathons with heated blankets and pizza."

"Bette Midler?"

"Yes," I answered, like duh. "*First Wives Club, Hocus Pocus*, and *Beaches*. My god."

He laughed and laughed. "Perfect."

"Oh, speaking of perfect. My little perfect paper flower is on my bookcase. And," I added, "as a florist, you might not want to hear this, but paper flowers just might be better than the real thing."

"How so?"

"Because they can't die. I'm keeping it forever, just so you know."

He sighed. "I'm torn. On one hand, hearing that makes me happy, but on the other hand, it's a knife to my poor little florist heart."

I couldn't help but laugh. "I feel like I should apologise. But the paper flower wins."

He sighed dramatically. "Well, that makes my decision about tomorrow much easier."

Wait. What?

"What do you mean? If I offended you— If you don't want—"

He barked out a laugh. "No! I was just trying to think what flowers I should give you for our first date—well, our first official, but actual second date. I was reading up on some Victorian floriography. I was trying to decide if I should go with funny." He sighed.

"Funny?"

"Yeah, like a larkspur. It kinda means *you're funny*."

I laughed but was still a little confused. "But now I'm not?"

"No. I mean, yes, you are. But no, now I think I'll bring you something else."

"You don't have to bring me anything. I don't expect anything."

"But I'm a florist. What kind of date would I be if I didn't bring you some kind of flower?"

"Yeah, but I don't expect you to bring me flowers every time you see me."

"Okay, see, here's the thing. If you were a baker and didn't bring me cookies or a cupcake every single time you saw me, I'd be sad."

I laughed. "Just as well I'm not a baker then. Considering you're already watching your cholesterol." But that got me thinking. "As a professional shopper, what can I bring you?"

"Nothing! I was just kidding."

"But you said you'd be sad."

"I was joking. Honestly." He chuckled and he sounded so warm and comfortable. "Maybe one day you can help me pick out some home décor. Not tomorrow. Another time, maybe."

I hummed, wondering if I should take that as an invitation. "I'd need to see your place first," I hedged. Then I cringed at myself for going there so soon. "Or you can show me photos, or whatever you're comfortable with. Do you live alone? Share a flat?"

"I live alone," he said. His tone was different. Lower, quieter. Like he'd read my offer for the invitation it was. "And I'd be comfortable with you seeing my place."

Well, damn.

For some stupid reason, I tried to play it cool. "Yeah, okay, sure. I'd be fine with that. Like tomorrow, even. If you want me to put together some ideas for your place. Some colour themes, mood boards, that kind of thing."

He laughed. "Mood boards? Do people really do that?"

"I do, yes. So my client can see which direction I'm going and veto anything they don't think is a suitable fit for their lifestyle."

"I'm more of a walk-into-Kmart-and-buy-whatever-I-find kind of client." He chuckled. "And it's not a work thing. I'm not your client. I'm your . . . date. So if you come back to my place, it won't be for work."

My stomach swooped, my nerves tingling with something that felt good. "Okay, date. Not work. I'm down with that. So, no mood boards then. Got it. I'll leave my colour swatch binder at home."

He made a happy sound. "I'm glad I called," he said softly. "I wasn't sure if I should."

"You absolutely should." I was smiling. I wasn't sure I'd stopped yet. "And I'm glad you did. And just so you know, I wouldn't mind seeing your place tomorrow anyway. As your date."

His breath in and groan on the exhale made my insides curl.

"I wouldn't mind that either," he said.

Oh, hell yes. He was definitely on the same page. "So, I'll see you tomorrow?"

"Yep. I'll be finished at the shop by one. I'll need to duck home and get changed."

"Oh, your work clothes are fine," I began.

"Well, if Robbie and Tan found out I went on two dates in my work clothes, they would kill me. And I'm not even exaggerating. Robbie's going to revoke my gay card when he finds out I went to dinner tonight with you whilst wearing my work uniform. He'll be horrified."

"Tell him it was my idea and that I made you do it."

He snorted. "Throwing you under the bus doesn't feel right."

"Well, don't worry if he does revoke your gay card. I'm sure I have a spare one somewhere."

"Thanks."

"Well, I should go. My show's almost over. I don't know what to watch next. *My Dream Home* or that sewing bee show."

"There's a sewing bee show?"

I gasped. "Okay, you're definitely not on my level of middle-aged gay. You need to get up to speed."

He laughed quietly. "I shall google. In the name of research. Will there be a quiz?"

"Absolutely."

"I'll look forward to it."

Yep. Still smiling. "See you tomorrow, Keats."

"Yes, you will."

I ended the call and hugged my cushion with the stupidest smile on my face, wiggling a little happy dance in my seat, resisting the urge to squeal, and thanking god that Cory couldn't see me now.

I did manage to get some work done in the morning, which was probably a good thing. I needed the distraction because while I sat on King's Wharf waiting for Keats to show up, I was heading into *overthinking* territory, which never ended well.

For anyone.

Especially Cory.

"What if I'm reading too much into this?" I asked him. "Actually, I'm pretty sure I am."

"Well, yesterday you said you found the man you're going to marry, so . . ."

"Right? Because . . . well, damn. I still think that today. Probably more today than I did yesterday."

"Oh dear."

"And I basically invited myself to his place," I added. "Why do I do this?"

"Because it's ingrained in you to please people. You want to be everything from the get-go."

True.

"So, should I play hard to get? Should I tell him sex is off the table until I'm sure?"

"Linden, I am the wrong person to ask that," he said flatly. "I'm the king of the nail and bail."

I snorted. "Yes, you are. More like the queen of the nail and bail. But okay."

"I'll allow that." He sighed. "If it feels right, do it."

"But it always feels right, does it not?"

"Well, it feels some kinda way."

"That's not helping."

"I say do it. Go back to his place and let him rail you. See if he's still the dream guy you think he is. If he's considerate, if he's any good, basically if he knows how to work you over. Because how are you going to spend your life with a guy who's bad in bed?" He made a disgusted sound. "It might be called same-sex marriage, but that doesn't mean it has to be the same sex over and over until the day you die."

"That's the reason I love you."

"And I love you. It really is a shame we're not compatible, you know."

I snorted. "Because we're both bottoms?"

"No, because your idea of a perfect date is a coffee date and trip to the plant section at Bunnings. Honestly, at this rate, I'm starting to question how we are even friends."

I rolled my eyes. "You'll find a guy who knocks you off your feet one day, and you'll be taking trips to IKEA and having picnics on the beach. Just you watch."

"Will he have a huge dick?"

"Knowing you, yes."

"Thank god."

"And he'll do something utterly corny like write you love notes on Post-its and you'll be a smitten kitten in your house with a picket fence and pet poodles."

"Say the words smitten kitten to me again and I'll call the police."

"I would, but they have handcuffs and I know you like that."

He laughed. "Have your lovesick date, and I want all the details, Linden. All of them. Is he there yet? I mean, he's not technically late, but still . . ."

I looked around, and sure enough, walking towards me was Keats. He wore faded aubergine trousers and a simple crewneck knitted sweater in grey and a smile that squeezed my heart. "Oh, here he is," I said into the phone. "Holy shit, Core, he's so hot."

"All the details," Cory said. "All of them."

I disconnected the call just as Keats got closer. "Hey," I said.

His smile became a grin. "Hey."

"You look great," I said. "Is this the new outfit?"

He looked down at himself. "Ah, yeah. One of them."

"Are the pants Todd Snyder?" I asked. I was sure they were.

"Um, I don't know who that is." He cringed. "They were kinda expensive."

I chuckled. "And the sweater, too."

"Probably. They took me to a lot of stores."

"Well, Robbie has great taste. They chose well for you."

"I'll tell him you said that."

"Though to be fair and completely honest with you, I like your work clothes just fine too. Pretty sure it wouldn't matter what you wear."

His smile was shy, his cheeks pink. Then he gestured to me. "And you look great, but you always do."

"Thanks."

"It's nice down here," he said, looking up and down the wharf. "Busy."

"It's always busy here, but this is one of my favourite coffee places." I pointed to the café nearby. "Are you familiar with Singaporean coffee?"

"Ah, no. But I'm down to try anything."

I raised an eyebrow. "That's good to know."

He blushed again, then cleared his throat before he let out a rush of air. "Right. Oh, before I forget." He reached into his pocket and pulled out a small, flat paper flower. "For you."

Oh my word.

I took it, feeling its surprising weight in my palm. It was white and had four flat petals. "Keats, oh my god, it's . . ."

"It's a white pansy."

My gaze shot to his. "White pansy. Is that a . . . a slur?"

His eyes went wide. "No!" Then he laughed. "No, no. Not at all. What?"

"Phew. I was having flashbacks to high school."

He laughed but it was soon a frown as he put his hand on my arm. "No, I'm sorry. A white pansy . . . So my origami skills aren't great and this one was kinda easy, and you said last night the paper flower I gave you was the best thing ever, so . . ."

"It was," I said. "It is . . . it's so pretty. And . . . I don't know what a white pansy means. Does it have a meaning?"

His eyes went to the flower and his cheeks flushed with more colour. "Of course. It means *think of me.*"

"Think of you?"

His gaze shot up and he nodded. "As often as I think of you."

Oh holy shit.

Maybe we could forego the coffee and just completely forget the shopping trip and just go straight back to his place.

"Uh, I already do," I managed, my voice a whisper. "Think of you, I mean. I don't know if it's as often as you think of me, but I'd probably guess it's equal to or more than. More than, probably. Definitely. I'm fairly sure it's more than. I think of you a lot." I offered him the flower. "Maybe you should take this and think of me more. So we can be even."

He chuckled. "Keep it. I have about fifty back at work."

"You do?"

"Yeah. I made a lot of practice ones. They weren't good enough; most ended up in the bin. Like I said, my origami skills are a bit rusty. Lina wanted to strangle me, and she'd have probably got more work done if I wasn't there at all today. But anyway, I finally made one that was good enough."

I pressed it flat to my chest, careful not to damage it. "Good enough? It's perfect. I'm going to keep it with the one from last night." Then I thought about that. "Just out of curiosity, what kind of flower was that last night?"

He laughed. "That was the only one I knew how to make off the top of my head. I'm not sure there's a floriography meaning."

"You could have totally lied to me," I said. "And told me it means sweetness or something, and I'd have totally believed you."

He squinted against the sun, smiling. "I'm really not the lying kinda guy, sorry."

I could see the honesty in his eyes, the gesture of this little flower in my hand. "I can see that, yeah."

I took a deep breath in and let it out slowly. I could try not to overthink this much, but he was just all kinds of incredible, and I wasn't sure there was much point in fighting it.

I nodded to the café. "So, coffee?"

He grinned. "Yes, please."

CHAPTER FIVE
KEATS

THE CAFÉ WAS AMAZING. A PLACE CALLED KOPI, A newish franchise popping up all over, and the fact I'd heard of it spoke of its popularity. It was the brainchild of a young Sydney guy who ran the company with his boyfriend, or maybe they were husbands now. Linden couldn't remember.

But he knew most of what went on.

"Gotta support our queer fam," he said. "And they're eco-responsible so it's a win-win."

And the coffee was great. So was the white-chocolate and raspberry-fudge cookie Linden put in front of me. "I might not be a baker, but I can always bring you a cookie. Believe me, you don't want me to bake it for you. But buy it for you, I can do."

We had the usual get-to-know-each-other conversation.

He was originally from Gosford. He had an older sister, and she and his mum still lived there. They were close and spoke every few days. He tried to get home to see them as often as he could, which, he admitted, wasn't as often as he'd like.

He hated school, never bothered with uni, and went

straight into PA work through an agency in the city. He was better with people than he ever was at studies, and his ability to read a person from their posture to their shoes was something akin to an FBI profiler.

I told him that.

"Or a personal shopper," he said with a laugh. "I love shopping and fashion, and I know what someone needs before they do."

"And what do I need?" I regretted saying that the second it was out of my mouth. "Sorry. Don't answer that."

He sipped his coffee. "Want me to tell you what you need?"

Not really.

"Um . . ."

He laughed. "You need me."

Well now. I wasn't expecting that.

"Oh. Is that right? I thought you were going to say something like a social life or a *Queer Eye* intervention."

He chuckled. "I think Robbie and Tan took care of that."

I winced. "A few outfits do not a new man make."

He smiled at that. "I like the old you just fine." Then he sighed. "But yes. I think you need me. For what greater purpose, I'm not sure yet. But I'm glad we're here."

I wasn't sure what to say. I also wasn't sure why my heart was thumping so erratically.

"So tell me," he went on. "What's the Keats McCulloch story?"

I took a deep breath in and exhaled slowly. "It's very boring, I'm afraid. I have a brother and a sister, both younger. My parents are still married. They live in Concord."

"Cool. They know you're gay?"

"Yep. Well, I didn't really come out until after high school. I'd been seeing a guy and kinda played it off as a friend who I hung out with but, clearly, I was never a good actor because my mum asked me to invite my boyfriend over for dinner so they could meet him. And that was that. I asked her about it later and she assumed I knew that they all knew I was gay. It was never discussed. It was just how it was."

Linden snorted. "Well, that's a good thing, right? They certainly weren't against it."

"Oh sure, it was a good thing. She also said the fact that in my high school days I would belt out George Michael songs in the shower was a bit of a sign, and that my teenage infatuation with shirtless Ricky Martin posters went above and beyond what would probably be classed as heteronormative."

He laughed. "Probably."

"But yes, they were fine with it. What about you? How was your family?"

"Well, my parents split when I was about two. My father stuck around for a few years of parental visits that were purely mandatory from *his* parents' part; apparently his mother made him. When I was about five, I was very clearly more fem than other boys. I liked my sister's dress-up games, and we'd play dolls and do make-up, and my dad told my mum it wasn't right. Long story short, she told him to never come back."

Damn.

"Ouch."

He braved a smile. "They had a million differences and a lot of other issues, not just me. And Mum could deal with him hating everything about her, but the second he tried that shit on five-year-old me, she was done. He wanted to still live as a single man without a wife and kids, and he bailed as soon as he could. So he was merely the donor, never a father, never a dad."

I nodded. "Your mum sounds great."

"She is. She's had a new boyfriend now for about five years. He's a nice guy. Treats her like a queen."

"I'm glad."

"And your first kiss? Boy or girl? And how terrible was it?"

I laughed. "I was in year ten at school, so fifteen, I guess? It was with a boy, and it was, without contest, terrible." I couldn't help but chuckle. "I mean, there were butterflies and that adrenaline rush of excitement, but it was more of a smashing of faces in the bathrooms at the movies."

He laughed. "I love that."

"I think he was mostly curious, whereas I totally knew I was into guys. He was my first unrequited love so it's kinda bittersweet."

"Aww, teen angst at its finest."

"Absolutely." I sipped my drink. "And what about your first kiss?"

"Oh, awkward and embarrassing. I was shaking so bad I thought he was going to jab me with an EpiPen."

I almost snorted coffee out of my nose.

He sighed and raised his chin, and if he'd had long hair, I'm sure he would have flicked it. "But he was also a huge creep. I was fourteen and he was eighteen."

"Ew."

"Yep. Back then I thought I was mature and all grown up. In hindsight, I can see I was still a child and he was a pervert."

"Ah, yes."

"I never did anything more with him than that one kiss, but it cemented my gaydom. There was no doubt after that," he added. Then he winced. "That I liked guys, not paedophiles."

I snorted. "Yes, I got that. But thanks for the clarification."

He smiled at me. "So, what's your ideal date?"

"April twenty-fifth."

He burst out laughing. "Great movie."

"Glad you got the reference." I ignored the fact my cheeks were burning. "Uh, I would say maybe this." I gestured between us, to the table, to the café. "This is kinda perfect for me."

He licked his lips before a smile won out. "This, for me as well. And maybe a trip to the garden centre?" His gaze held mine. "Then maybe we'd take the plants back to my place and you can show me the best place to keep them. You know, for optimum sunlight positioning, that kind of thing."

Right, then.

Back to his place. And from the look in his eyes, he wasn't talking about the plants.

I nodded slowly, trying not to appear too eager. "Sounds like a solid plan."

His smile was shy and the tips of his ears were red. Yep, we were definitely on the same page.

"We don't have to find the closest Bunning's though," I added. "The Botanic Gardens have a nursery shop. We could go take a look if you want?"

"The Botanic Gardens?" His whole face brightened. "How did I not know they have a plant shop? I haven't been there in years. It's so pretty up there."

"It is. I haven't been in a while either. It'll be fun."

He finished his coffee. "Ready to take me plant shopping?"

"As I'll ever be."

The truth was, I'd never been more excited for any kind of shopping. And for what might be happening later back at his place. I was trying not to think about that and instead focused on enjoying every moment.

After all, taking a gorgeous man plant shopping in the

Botanic Gardens on a lovely spring day was in itself a highlight for me. Not even a perfect date, but a truly perfect day.

THE NURSERY ITSELF WAS QUAINT AND RUSTIC, something out of a romance movie. And as soon as Linden walked inside, I wondered if it was a bad idea.

He gasped loudly and gripped my arm. "Oh my god, look at all the baby plants! I want one of everything!"

I didn't even mind him calling them baby plants because his eyes were as wide as his grin, and he kept his hand on my arm.

"Look at this one," he said, excitedly showing me a Sydney red gum sapling. "He looks like a Harold."

"A Harold?"

"Yes, his name."

"Oh, I, uh . . . I wasn't aware plants had names."

"Of course they do."

I laughed. "Right, yes, of course. So, will Harold be living inside or outside at your place?"

"Inside. I have a balcony but it's tiny."

"Then maybe we should look at the inside plants and not the ones that grow to about thirty metres."

"Oh. Probably a very good idea. Sorry, Harold."

Yes, sorry, Harold.

We wandered over to the indoor section, his arm now linked through mine. It made me ridiculously happy. I picked up a small seedling. "You mentioned a pothos before. This one is similar. Well, it will be when it's bigger."

"He's so teeny." He gently touched the new leaf. "He's barely a sprout."

"He will grow."

Linden began to smile. "So he's a grower, not a show-er."

I rolled my eyes but couldn't help but laugh. "I think he is, yes."

"Then he shall be coming home with me."

"Does he get a name?"

He looked at the plant and nodded. "Sprout."

I chuckled. "How did you go from Harold to Sprout?"

"Because . . . well, because that's the names that come to me when I look at them."

"Right. Okay then."

"Are you judging my naming abilities, Mr Keats Perfect-Name McCulloch? Because believe me, when you grow up with the name of a retirement home, you fully appreciate the importance of a name."

I snorted. "No judgement here at all. I happen to think the name Sprout is cute. And my middle name isn't Perfect-Name. And you don't have the name of a retirement home."

"It's either a retirement home, or an abandoned asylum for the insane that was shut down in the 1960s for shady practices. Those are the only two options a name like Linden Acres could ever procure, and I was going with the nicer option of a retirement home than the horror movie location haunted asylum."

I laughed again. "Like the kind of movie where the teenagers dare each other to camp out overnight."

"Exactly."

"Then the retirement home is probably the nicer option, even though I don't agree with those two options."

"Could there possibly be a third? A toilet freshener, perhaps."

I snorted. "No. I like your name."

"You're a terrible liar."

"I'm not lying!"

"Your pants should totally be on fire right now." Then he side-eyed me. "You mentioned a middle name. What's yours?"

"Joseph."

"Keats Joseph McCulloch," he said as if he was trying it on for size. "Perfect."

"Joseph was my grandfather. What's your middle name?"

He groaned. "I don't like this game."

I laughed. "It can't be that bad."

"Francis," he said flatly. "Linden Francis Acres."

Oh.

"And I don't even have the excuse that it was some great grandfather's name. My parents just suck at naming things. My sister's name is Odelia. And my mum has a cat called Ceefa."

"Cee for cat?"

"Naturally. I guess I should be grateful my name isn't Beebeefa. You know, bee for baby boy."

"Small blessings, huh?"

"Very small." He held up the tiny plant. "Like Sprout." Then he looked at a fern. "Ooh, I like this one too. How big will she grow?"

It was a maidenhair fern and apparently a she. "She'll grow better if she's hanging or on a windowsill. Her limbs and leaves will hang down."

"Like Rapunzel?" He smiled at the plant. "Rapunzel, I love you already."

I grinned at him. I had to wonder if I'd stopped yet. "Perfect."

"Now you have to pick one for your place. And give it a name. No pressure to be as cool as mine though."

I looked at the tables of plants and found a philodendron. "This one," I declared.

Linden pouted. "Yours is bigger than my little Sprout."

"Should I get a seedling too, so they can grow at the same time?"

He picked up a tiny pot with a seedling the same size as his and grinned as he handed it to me. "This one. They can go to little plant day care together."

I laughed. This was so absurd . . . and so much fun. "Deal."

"And a name?"

I looked at the little plant, which really was no more than a sprout. "Hmm, she looks like an Elizabeth."

"Oh, okay, wow."

"Is there something wrong with the name Elizabeth?"

"No, it's perfect. I just wasn't expecting such a traditional name." He looked around. "I think I want a bigger one too. One that's more established so it creates the aesthetic I want. As cute as little Sprout is, and I'm sure he'll grow up big and strong. But I want greenery."

I showed him a bigger version. "Like this one?"

"Yes, perfect. And this one," he said, pointing to a calathea. "It's really pretty."

"Okay, names first."

"Hmm," he said, studying the bigger pothos seriously. "Leonardo."

Okay then. "Uh, the artist or the Ninja Turtle?" Then I considered something else. "Or DiCaprio?"

He laughed. "I was going with da Vinci, but the Ninja Turtle could work."

I lifted the frond on the calathea. "And this one?"

"He's a Peter for sure."

I snorted. Of course he was a Peter.

I found a nice rotundifolia. "And I'll take this one too."

"And the name?"

"Sebastian."

"Elizabeth and Sebastian. Nice."

"Are you mocking my name choices?"

He put his hand to his heart. "Absolutely not. But what I am saying is that if we ever get a cat, I shall be the one naming it."

Oh my god.

"Really? You have us getting a cat together?" I tried not to smile too big, though the way my heart pinballed happily against my ribs made it difficult. "Good to know."

He sniffed but his cheeks bloomed a lovely shade of pink. "Maybe. Hypothetically."

"And pray tell, what would you name our cat? Hypothetically."

"I'd need to see it first. But probably Professor Meatball."

I snorted out a laugh. "Okay, well, that's a very boyish name. What if it's a girl cat?"

He shrugged. "Professor Spaghetti. I think we'd need two cats."

I laughed. "Meatball and Spaghetti. That's actually . . . perfect."

He beamed, then looked at the plants we'd collected. "Well, we better get these home." Then the corner of his mouth pulled down with uncertainty. "Did you still want to come back to my place, or . . . ?"

I didn't know why he seemed so unsure. "Uh, considering we just named our hypothetical future cats, I think I should, yes."

His eyes met mine and he pulled his bottom lip between his teeth to rein in his smile. "Seems fair."

We paid for our new plants, loaded them into a box, and I

carried it. He booked us an Uber, and a few minutes later, he was unlocking his front door and holding it open for me.

It was a small unit but very nicely decorated. He had very good taste and everything matched, from the couch to the coffee table and TV stand and bookcase. He had pictures on the walls in frames that matched the furniture.

"Great place," I said, sliding the box of plants onto his kitchen counter. "You have style and impeccable taste."

"It's more a case that I have a flair for knowing what's on sale and when to buy it," he replied.

"No, this is stylish. My decoration style is more college-dorm with a splash of op-shop vibe." I laughed, but I wasn't kidding. "I really do need someone to take me shopping and tell me what to get."

He put his hand to his chest. "Like me?"

I met his gaze. "I don't want you to think of me as work!"

He stepped in close and softly pressed his lips to mine.

It was far too unexpected, far too brief. I leaned in for more, high on the thrill of that kiss . . . but he pulled back, smiling. Teasing.

"Believe me, I don't," he said. "Think of you as work, that is."

My heart, which I was pretty sure had almost stopped, kick-started with a bang inside my chest. I felt a little dizzy. He, on the other hand, was still smiling and coherent enough to start taking his plants out of the box.

"Oh look, little Sprout, this is your new home," he said, popping him on the kitchen windowsill. "And Leonardo, my friend, you're going over here." He put him on the bookcase near the window. "Will he get enough sunlight here?" he asked me.

I was still stuck on that kiss. "Uh, sure."

Linden chuckled and brought over a small plate, and I

realised it had the two paper flowers on it. He took the one I'd given him today from his pocket and pinched the edges a little. "It got a little squished," he said.

"You're really keeping those," I said.

His gaze shot to mine. "They are the best thing I've ever been given. Of course I'm keeping them."

"Then I'll make you one every time we meet."

He walked over and slid the small plate onto the counter, and when his eyes met mine, there was a different light in them. "I really want to kiss you again," he said.

"I'm still kinda caught up on the last one," I said. "It was far too brief."

He made a sound that was half a laugh, half a groan. "It was all I dared to do," he whispered. "Keats, if I kiss you right now, I will want more. I will want you to take me to bed and I don't know if you want that, or if you think it's too soon."

Holy shit.

My knees were feeling a little wobbly, my chest was far too tight. But my blood . . . my blood was running hot.

"I want that," I managed to say. "It probably is too soon, but you've already named our hypothetical cats, so—"

He slid his hand around my neck and pulled me in for a kiss. Soft lips, open and inviting, he pressed himself against me, leaning into me, and slipping his tongue into my mouth.

I heard the most guttural sound, and so god help me, I thought it came from me.

I wrapped my arms around him, and no one had ever felt this right against me. His small frame was perfect in every way, and he was soft planes and hard muscles and hard . . .

Jesus.

He was hard.

I ran my hand down over his arse and pulled his hips flush

with mine. I wanted him to feel I was as turned on as him. That he was doing this to me.

He broke the kiss, panting, his eyes heavy-lidded and his lips swollen. "Bedroom?"

I nodded. "Yes, please."

He took my hand and led me down a short hall to his bedroom. He turned and pulled me in for another kiss, and he let me take control. He wanted me to take charge, to do him how I wanted.

It was a constant war between urgency and hot-blooded desire and the need to show him the restraint and perfection he deserved.

I tried for the latter.

I ran my hand up his chest, to his throat, and with my fingertip under his chin, I tilted his face upward so I could kiss him. I delved my tongue deep into his mouth, tangling and tasting and trying to pace myself.

When he surrendered to me, I pulled his shirt over his head and tossed it, then pulled my sweater off too. With my hand cupping his jaw, I kissed him again and pushed him until he backed onto the bed, and I gently lowered him down.

I let my body weight press him into the mattress as I kissed him, and he instinctively widened his legs and raised his hips. His desperation began to show in the way he clawed at my back as he rolled his hips.

This was going to be over way too fast.

I pulled back and went to my haunches between his thighs hoping for a second to calm down, but it only made it worse. "Holy shit, you look so hot right now."

His thin, pale torso and the bulge in his jeans.

"I'm trying to pace myself," I admitted. "Or this'll be over before it begins."

He laughed, his tongue poking out at the corner of his

lips. "Maybe we should make this the first course," he said, his eyes raking down my chest to the very noticeable erection in my trousers. He grunted and arched his back. "Yeah, starters first, main course later."

I took his leg and tried to take his shoe off. "No time for that," he said, undoing his jeans and pulling his dick out. "I'm not kidding, Keats."

I grinned at him, popped the button on my pants, and undid my fly. I freed my cock, groaning at the contact. "Glad we're on the same page."

"Holy fuck," he breathed, his eyes on my dick. "Oh, Keats, yes please."

I leaned forward, one hand pressed to the mattress beside his head, quickly taking both our erections in my other hand. Hot and hard, silky and slick with precome. Linden's eyes rolled back in his head, his hips raised.

He was breathtaking. So sensual, so sexy, with his flushed cheeks and pink lips.

And he felt so, so good.

He was rocking his hips, meeting my fist with every thrust, and it was too much. He was too hot, I was too turned on, and it'd been far too long. This pleasure, this emotion, was a ticking bomb, getting closer and closer . . .

He cried out, his body jerking beneath me, and it was all it took for my orgasm to detonate inside me. I came in spurts up his stomach and chest, just one moment before he did the same. His body arched underneath me, his cock pulsing against mine. My whole body trembled; every cell burned with ecstasy as I tried to keep my weight off him.

Smiling, he put his hands to my face and pulled me down for a kiss, and when I collapsed on top of him, he laughed. "Well, the first course was delicious," he said, his voice gravelly and warm. "Second course is going to be even better."

I chuckled, my face in his neck. "Might need a few minutes."

Or maybe thirty.

He hummed happily, his hands exploring up my back, slowly bringing me back into reality. To the sticky mess now smeared between us. I propped my head up on my hand so I could look into his eyes. "We should probably get showered." I made no attempt to move off him. I wasn't sure I could.

He laughed. "Or we could just stay right here." He ran his finger over my forehead, brushing my hair back, then down my jaw to my lips. His gaze followed the movement, and he chewed on his bottom lip. "I have specific requirements for the second course of this meal," he said.

I hummed and quirked an eyebrow. "Is that right?"

His lazy smile widened, and his eyes focused on mine. "Yep. I'm going to need a very thorough fucking."

I snorted, too blissed out to be shocked or embarrassed. "Is that right?"

"Yep. Now that I've actually seen your dick, I'm going to need more of it. Deep, and preferably frequently."

I laughed. "I'll be happy to oblige."

I had a fairly decent dick. Seven inches long with a fat mushroom head. Perfect for setting off some internal fire-works, apparently.

"Let me get you cleaned up," I said, peeling our stomachs apart from where we'd glued ourselves together.

"Shower," he suggested, sitting up. He drew a swirl in the drying come on his stomach. "God, this is hot, not gonna lie."

I got to my feet and held out my hand for his, then pulled him to his feet and followed him into his bathroom. We kicked off our shoes and pants, stumbled into the shower stall together, letting our soapy hands wander as we laughed into each kiss.

And never once did the butterflies stop. Never once did the thrill of each kiss subside, the anticipation, the nerves, the full swoop of my whole heart when he laughed.

Every touch, every caress, every breath.

One official date, one full afternoon with him, and I was in over my head. Okay, so I'd known him a month. We'd technically had two dates, we'd texted, we'd flirted. But one day with him and I knew . . . I just honestly knew.

I would absolutely let him name our cats Meatball and Spaghetti.

CHAPTER SIX
LINDEN

OH BOY.

Things were moving fast, yet somehow entirely not fast enough. I wanted everything with him, and I wanted it right now.

He wasn't perfect. No person was. But oh boy, he was perfect for me.

With his perfect name, his perfect face, his perfect job, his perfect laugh, and his perfect every-fucking-thing.

And his dick?

Perfection.

And I wasn't letting him leave until I'd had it inside me.

I needed it.

I mean, I wasn't holding him hostage, exactly. I was simply encouraging him to stay.

We'd showered and re-dressed, and after I had Keats show me how to make sure the new plants were adequately watered, I suggested a snack and some Netflix. He readily agreed and then we were on the couch, and twenty minutes later, his attention lasered in on me.

He pressed his shoulder to mine, closer. His body heat was heavenly. Electric.

He angled his face so all I could see was the sharpness of his jaw and the column of his neck.

I wanted to lick every inch of him.

His thumb traced lines across my thigh, sliding inward. Upward.

Then he made a low groan, almost a grunt, and I was about to burst into flames.

I turned side on. "Are you trying to kill me?"

He chuckled, his dark eyes full of promise and desire. "I've never wanted anyone the way I want you," he murmured. "It's all I can think about, and you're so close but nowhere near close enough."

Oh boy.

"Spontaneous combustion is a thing, I'll have you know," I said, my voice much breathier than I'd intended. "I'm very close to ignition, so if you have no intention of taming this fire, I might suggest you stop."

He smirked and drew his hand further up the inside of my thigh, sliding, seeking, and steaming hot. "I don't want to stop," he breathed. His gaze met mine and the heat in his stole my breath. "I want to take you back to bed."

I nodded, woodenly at first, then as though my head might wobble right off my shoulders. "Do you intend to fuck me?" I murmured. Somehow my voice worked. Barely.

He leaned in, his nose drawing up my jaw, and he whispered in my ear. "Is that what you want?"

"Yes," I said, far too quickly. My entire body felt charged, buzzing, and I wondered if spontaneous combustion was actually a thing.

I snatched up his hand, pulled him to his feet, and all but dragged him back to my bed. I pulled my shirt over my head and undid my jeans, trying to undress as fast as I could . . .

While he stood there and watched.

Like he was watching a gift unwrap itself.

Until he stilled my hand. He licked the corner of his mouth and swallowed hard as his gaze raked down my body and back up to my face. He skimmed his fingertips over my chest, drawing goosebumps in their wake, over my nipple, and when he reached my neck, he cupped my jaw, his thumb on my chin.

He tilted my face upward and crushed his mouth to mine, all lips and tongue, demanding.

And I let him.

In that moment, I would've let him do whatever the hell he wanted to me.

He was in charge; he was in control.

I fucking loved it.

He sucked on my tongue and ran his hands down my back, over my arse, and pushed my jeans down to the floor.

Hell yes.

But he was still dressed, and I needed him to be as naked as me.

I tugged at the hem of his sweater and he did the honours of pulling it off, then I fumbled with the button on his pants. He took my face in his hands and kissed me while I got his pants undone and pushed them down, and finally—finally— he was as naked as me.

His gorgeous dick jutting out proudly, pressing against me, the thick round head smearing precome on my belly.

I couldn't wait to have it inside me.

He slowed the kiss, his forehead to mine, his eyes closed. "Please tell me you have condoms."

I chuckled. "Top drawer, bedside."

He sighed, a smile tugging on his lips. "Lie down on the bed, on your belly."

My skin prickled all over and my balls drew down.

He took my chin between his thumb and forefinger. "Spread your legs for me."

Christ.

My knees felt like jelly, and I scrambled to do as he instructed. When I was face down and raised my hips to get my dick in a comfortable position, a bottle of lube and a foil packet hit the mattress beside me.

Oh hell yes.

The bed dipped and he ran his hands up the backs of my thighs as he came to kneel between my legs. I instinctively raised my hips and slid my hand underneath me to fist my cock.

"You want this as bad as I do, huh," he murmured. He held my hips before he pressed tender kisses at the base of my spine. His fingernails biting into my skin, his hot breath and soft lips almost too much and nowhere near enough.

"Keats," I mumbled, pressing my forehead into the mattress. I tried to give him more of my arse, tried to make him hurry.

I heard the muted click of the bottle lid, and even the cool drizzle of lube did little to quench the fire. When he ran his thumb over my hole, I thought the sparks might catch fire, but it still wasn't enough.

Not even when he probed his slick fingers into me.

It just felt like he was adding more fuel to dry kindling and tinder when all I wanted him to do was hurry up and light the fucking match.

"Keats," I said again, frustrated and desperate. "Stop playing with me. I need you to fuck me. Now."

He chuckled.

He thought this was funny?

I was just about to give him a piece of my mind when he took my legs and flipped me over.

I don't even know how.

But I was suddenly on my back with my legs up to my chest and he was leaning over me, his massive cockhead pressed against my arsehole. His face an inch from mine.

"Impatient?" he asked, the devil in his smirk.

Before I could answer, he pushed into me and I immediately regretted my urgency.

Holy shit.

Holy mother of god.

He pushed in until my body accepted his thick cockhead, the stretch giving way to a slow glide, and I could finally breathe.

Keats shuddered with restraint, his eyes squinted closed. "Oh my god," he breathed. Then his eyes shot open, the fire in them flickering with concern. "Are you okay?"

I managed to nod. "I am now. The head of your cock . . . holy fuck."

He shuddered again and pulled back and then drove up into me, slow and sure. "You're really tight. Oh, god." Then he kissed me, soft at first, then deeper, his tongue in my mouth keeping time with his thrusts.

He filled me so completely. Every inch, every space, every breath.

He rocked me, pushing my legs higher, pushing in deeper, and when he drove upwards, it struck something inside me.

Something magical and frightening.

I gasped, my hips bucking, but he pinned me right there—right fucking there—and he struck that place again.

I needed more of it, over and over, and I gripped his arse. "More. Right there. More." My voice didn't even sound like mine. It was fraught and desperate and pleading. "Please. More, please."

And he gave me more. Harder and repeatedly, striking that magical spot, tapping it like a flint against stone, sparks flying in all directions until finally—finally—the tinder caught alight.

A fire of pleasure so hot, so bright, ripped through me and consumed me.

All I could do was hold on and let him control the flames.

And control me, he did.

I'd never experienced anything like it. An orgasm so ferocious it felt like an out-of-body experience. So intense, so encompassing.

Somewhere in the haze I heard Keats groan, his striking that magical fire reaching a crescendo before he thrust in hard one last time, stilled, and cried out.

But I was lost to it, to him, to whatever the hell that was.

He collapsed on top of me, and neither one of us could move.

I was still so jittery, my nerves a frazzled mess, yet somehow sated and content, and . . .

And he slipped out of me.

It felt wrong to miss him when he was still on top of me, but I wanted him inside me again.

I wanted him always.

"You need to do that again," I said. "Repeatedly, forever. I don't even know what that was or if it was even legal, but I want more."

He chuckled lazily into my neck then rolled off me, collecting me and pulling me into his strong arms. My face pressed against his chest and he kissed the side of my head. "I would also like more," he mumbled. "But I'm gonna need a minute."

"Just a minute?"

He snorted. "Yeah, maybe an hour. Or two."

I was still twitchy, and when I clenched my arse, a full body shudder rippled through me. "Jesus."

He laughed and rubbed my back, and after a minute or two, my tremors settled and I began to feel heavy. "Feel better?"

"Hmm."

What I was feeling now was sleepy.

Wiped out, even.

He tightened his hold on me, and we dozed off.

I'd never felt so comfortable and safe in my entire life. Which was ridiculous, given the brief length of time I'd known Keats. I'd never even needed to feel safe before. But that's what I felt with him.

It was irrational and absurd, yet so very real.

And maybe it was the fact he'd just given me the best orgasm of my life—and I would hazard a guess that played a very big part—but my heart was already invested in him.

And when I woke to soft circles being traced on my back, gentle touches and sweet kisses to my forehead, I was in total agreement with my heart.

Doomed. By the second date. Well and truly in over my head, and I'd never been happier.

"I'm hungry," he murmured. "Shall we order in?"

I smiled, liking far too much that he didn't want to leave just yet. "Sounds good. What do you feel like?"

He sighed as he rubbed my back. "Chicken souvlaki, salad, and fries."

I laughed and sat up so I could see his face. "That was very specific."

He grinned. "You did ask. What do you feel like?"

"Chicken souvlaki, salad, and fries. Now that you mention it."

Now he laughed. "Perfect. I know a place."

He ordered it and we got dressed, falling onto the couch, my head on his chest, his arm around me, and we watched the end of some black-and-white movie.

It was crazy that we were comfortable with each other from the very start. I felt like I'd known him for years, not weeks. Yet, I still knew so very little about him.

"What music do you have on your playlists?" I asked.

"A mix, mostly. I have easy chill music for my store, though we tend to take it in turns. What's yours?"

"Depends on my mood. My middle-aged-gay era is leaning toward a lot of musical soundtracks."

"Bold choice."

I chuckled. "Name of your bucket-list concert?"

"Are we playing twenty questions?"

"Yes. I'm trying to find a flaw."

He laughed. "A flaw? I have many."

"Name them."

He groaned a drawn-out, almost-pained sound. "Jeez. Um. I get fixated."

"Like a stalker?"

He laughed again. "No. God, no. I mean with my work. My business is my priority."

I sat up, took his hand, and met his eyes. "It should be. It's your dream, right?"

He nodded.

"Then you should prioritise it. It's also your income and financial investment. It should be a priority. I'm sorry your ex didn't see that."

He squeezed my hand and studied my fingers for a long moment. "Thank you." Then he sighed. "Maybe you won't see it that way when you want to do something one day and I can't go with you."

"Thinking about our future?"

His gaze shot to mine. "Oh, well no. I didn't mean . . . I just meant hypothetically speaking . . . should we make it that far."

I laughed, and lifting our joined hands to my lips, I kissed his knuckles. "I already named our hypothetical future cats, remember?"

A smile won out. "Meatball and Spaghetti. How could I forget? And just so you know, I'm one hundred percent okay with you naming our hypothetical future cats."

I sighed, trying to ignore the way my heart was thrumming. "And just so *you* know, I've never named hypothetical cats with anyone before. Never even came close."

His smile was sweet and a little uncertain. "It's crazy, right? This? I don't know why it feels so right with you. And maybe it is way too premature to be admitting that. I thought maybe because it'd been a while since anyone had taken an interest in me . . ." Then he grimaced. "Well, that's not true. Since I've taken an interest in anyone."

"Oh, so there have been guys sniffing around," I said, kinda joking, kinda not. "Believe me, if you did to them what you did to me in bed, I'm not surprised they were trying to reel you in."

He grinned, though he was a little embarrassed. "They could sniff around all they liked. I was never interested. I had my shop and accounts to manage, finances to go over. It never ends."

"And now?"

Good one, Linden. Just ask him outright.

He smiled and watched our hands as he played with my

fingers. "And now I'm ready," he said quietly. Then his eyes met mine. "Because now there's you."

Oh boy.

My stomach swooped and my heart skipped several beats. "Because now there's you," I whispered back to him, the sweetest words anyone had ever said to me. "It is crazy, and it is fast. But it feels right, doesn't it?"

He nodded, then leaned over and kissed me softly. "Glad we're on the same page."

His phone beeped with the food delivery, and we ate our food sitting on the floor with the coffee table between us. It was fun, and it gave me a little distance.

There was a voice in my head telling me to find some perspective. A reality check, even.

I took a mouthful of chicken and salad and pointed my fork at him. "I'm still trying to find some flaws. You can't be this perfect."

"I'm not perfect," he said, shaking his head. "Please don't think I am. You'll only be disappointed."

"You said you had many flaws. Name some."

He shoved some fries in his mouth and spoke around them. "Want me to talk with my mouth full?"

I laughed. "No."

He laughed as he chewed and swallowed. "Okay, so for the last few years, it's just been me. I haven't had to consider anyone else, so I'm assuming I'm selfish to some degree."

"Ah, but the fact you're aware of it and consider it to be a flaw puts you ahead of the game. Next."

He grinned. "Sometimes I leave my plates in the sink overnight and don't wash up until after breakfast."

"Oh no," I joked. "That's a deal breaker right there."

He rolled his eyes and stabbed a piece of chicken. "Okay, honestly, this one's a big one, and I should be ashamed, but

I'm glad this chicken died for us to eat it because it's delicious."

I barked out a laugh. "Oh my god, the cruelty."

He smiled at me, then it faded slowly. "I don't know what my flaws are. Maybe I'm not as self-aware as I should be."

"Then what's a deal breaker for you? What's something that if I did it, you'd be gone?"

"Lying," he replied. "If you lie to me, about anything. I'd rather hear a harsh truth than a cushioned lie."

"Fair enough."

"Cheating," he added.

"Oh yes, agree one hundred percent. Arsehole ex Jason, remember?"

He made a face. "Oh, sorry. I didn't mean to bring that up. It was kinda covered in the no-lying clause. Sorry."

I waved him off. "Don't worry about it. I'm well and truly over that jerk. He did me a favour, because if he hadn't cheated on me, I wouldn't have walked into your store looking for murder flowers."

He smiled at me. "Maybe I should thank him."

"Well, I wouldn't go that far."

He laughed quietly. "What's another deal breaker for you? Aside from the lying and cheating."

"If we went out somewhere and you were rude to the sales staff or wait staff, like if you spoke down to them, that'd be a deal breaker for me," I admitted. "No one is better than anyone else, regardless of job title or wealth."

He smiled. "I like that. And as someone who is in customer service, I totally agree."

"You deal with horrible people?"

"All the time."

I scrunched my nose up. "It's so gross. I'm honestly surprised I don't see it more, given my line of work. I deal with some incredibly wealthy people and they've all been fairly decent so far. I mean, they might be complete douches and be horrible people in general, but they're nice to me and any other staff I've seen them interact with. Though there was one woman, an Instagram fitness influencer of all things. I met her for a prelim, to see if we could work together, and she made her young assistant cry in front of me. She was a nasty piece of work. I told her she wasn't anyone I would associate my name with and walked out. I won't stand for it."

He seemed pleased about this. "Good for you."

"And I guess someone who wanted to be in my life would need to meet Cory. He's my best friend. He tried to tell me that my ex was trash, and I should have listened. Plus, Jason never liked Cory and that should have been a sign. I guess I just wanted to see something that wasn't there." I smiled at Keats. "Remember what you said to me after you helped me deliver those flowers to him?"

His gaze met mine. "I said you deserved better."

"You did. And I do." I nodded slowly. "And I think I found him."

His smile was slow and warm, his eyes full of sincerity. "Maybe I should meet Cory. You know, just to be sure."

Jeez, I had to drag Jason kicking and screaming to meet him, and here Keats was volunteering. Proof that I'd definitely found myself a good one.

My heart felt two times too big for my chest. "Maybe you should."

"HE WANTS TO MEET YOU," I SAID.

Cory and I were doing our weekly Sunday afternoon catch-up. No matter how busy our weeks were, we always made time for each other. Sometimes it was running errands; sometimes trips to a dry cleaner or laundromat. Sometimes it was a trip to his family or mine. Today's catch-up was groceries in Woolworths.

He stopped pushing his trolley. "Meet me? Already?"

"I know! I'm telling you, Core, he's different. The man is a walking green flag. Well, at least I think he is. I need you to tell me what I'm not seeing. I mean, he's perfect." I had to stop using that word. "Well, he's perfect for me."

"You slept with him already?"

"Wow. Judgement is in aisle five, okay? We're only in aisle two."

He rolled his eyes. "You know I'm not judging you." He put his manicured hand to his chest. "Darling, I am no one to judge. I haven't told you about what happened last night yet. But I know you. You sleep with them and you catch feelings."

"You sleep with random men and catch—"

A woman walked past and gave us the stink eye.

"Judgement is in aisle five," Cory told her.

I took his hand and pulled him away before he could get into a smack down with Stink Eye Susan and her basket full of plant-based tofu. Christ. Did she even know what tofu was?

Marketing really preyed on the stupid.

I looked up and down the mostly empty aisle. "It wasn't just sex. It was . . ." I shook my head and tried to keep my voice down. "Cory, it was so much more. It was the best sex of my life. I can't even describe it."

His eyes lit up. "How good?"

"Is it possible for his dick to shoot meth or cocaine? Because I'm seriously addicted after one time. I need more of whatever the fuck he did to me. I'm not even kidding. Do fat mushroom-headed cocks have some magic-mushroom jizz?"

Cory roared, laughing so loud that the man at the end of the aisle stopped and stared. "Yeah, I think I would have heard about that before now. Or had it myself."

"I'm not joking, Cory. Imagine a huge firework rocket. Now douse it in petrol, add some sparkles for funsies, then set it on fire. That's what he did to me."

He leaned in and did some weird thing with his eyebrows. "It sounds like you had a prostate orgasm."

"Have you ever had one?"

"Once."

"And?"

"It was a firework rocket doused in petrol with sparkles for funsies and set on fire."

"And you never told me about this because . . ."

"If I told you about every sexual encounter I have, we'd never talk about anything else."

I considered that and relented a nod. "True." Then I spotted some brown rice crackers over his shoulder and grabbed a packet. "Ooh, I need some of these."

Cory pushed the trolley and we started up the aisle. "And he wants to meet me? Already?"

"I know it's too soon. I mean, I already named our hypothetical cats, and that was before he did the magic-mushroom-head-dick thing."

Cory stopped walking. "You named what?"

"Our future children."

He made a face that was pure aghast. "Your *what*?"

He was also clutching his heart. "I love that nail colour, by the way."

He inspected his nails. "Oh, thanks. It's called Atomic Tangerine. Now please explain the children thing."

"Cats, not human children." I shuddered. "Meatball and Spaghetti."

"Have mercy, you do have it bad."

"I told you after day one that I'd met the man I was going to marry. I don't know why you're surprised."

He studied me for a few long seconds, then nodded. "Hm. Fine. I'll meet him. What am I looking for, exactly?"

"Anything. You know I'm blind to these things."

"Yes, the love goggles."

"And after Jason . . ."

"I told you he was a slimy douche."

"And I'll listen this time."

Cory sighed. "Linden, you're my best friend and I love you."

Oh dear . . .

"But you've never listened, not once. And I've been right every single time."

"I know."

"And if I tell you there's something up with Mr Perfect, father of your future cat children, what will you do?"

"Cry." I shrugged and tried to think of what I'd actually do. "No, that's it. I'd cry and be heartbroken and sad for all eternity."

"Oh great." He threw up his hands and went back to pushing the trolley. "No pressure then."

I stood there in the middle of the aisle until I noticed the pita crackers that were *so* good with hummus. I grabbed a packet and had to power walk to catch up to Cory.

"So, tell me about last night," I said.

He turned, holding a box of cold-brew sachets. "Oh my god." He threw the box into the trolley and took a jar of coffee from the shelf. It was cylindrical and he couldn't get his hand around it. "This big, I'm telling you. I thought I was going to split in half."

I took the coffee from him and gave the poor woman with unfortunate timing an apologetic smile. "Jesus, Cory."

He was undeterred. "It was so good. So much better this time around."

"Wait . . . *This* time?"

Cory smirked and gave a smug sniff. Then he held up three fingers. "Third time."

"With the same guy?" I might have shrieked that, so I tried again much quieter and with less astonishment. "You had a repeat with the same guy?"

The fact it was three times was beside the point. He never did the same guy twice. Ever. But three times?

"And you never told me this?" I was dumbfounded. "Details, Cory. Now."

He laughed. "Remember that stallion that offered full servicing?"

"Yes. With the . . ." I held up the jar of coffee.

"His name is Amon. He's Egyptian. Well, his parents are. He was born here."

"Wait. You know details? You had a personal conversation with him?" I had to lean against the shelving. "Oh my god."

He gave me a shove. "Oh, shut up. I've spoken to the others. Sometimes. Like, once or twice."

Oh, please. He was lucky to ever even get a name.

"And you've met this Amon at the same bar three times? Deliberately?"

"First time was when I was with you. Never seen him before then. Second time was maybe lined up, and third time was at his place." He was fighting a smile. "After he took me out for dinner."

A date?

"A date?" I might have shrieked that too. "You went out on a date and you didn't think to tell me?"

"I am telling you right now. The date was last night," he replied. "And you and I have been here for all of twenty minutes and we haven't stopped talking about you long enough to get to me."

That stopped me.

All indignation deflated. "That's true. Sorry." I frowned at him. "I'm a shitty friend, sorry."

"You're not. You're the bestest friend ever." He began walking again and I hurried to fall into step with him. "I thought you were sworn off men for all eternity."

"I was. Until him."

He plucked a bottle of probiotics from the health food shelf. "Here. You're going to need these for all the magic-mushroom dick you'll be getting."

I took the bottle and smiled at a guy who was looking at vitamin pills but now took a sidestep away from us.

"What?" Cory asked him. "Gut health is important."

I took his arm and led him down the aisle. "Leave the unsuspecting straight population alone. Oh, I need some muesli."

Shopping done, we headed back to my place first to drop off my groceries. "Are you sure you don't mind helping?" Cory asked.

"Are you kidding? Cleaning out wardrobes and ensuring you make the best possible fashion choices is my favourite thing to do."

We climbed the stairs to my floor and there in front of my door was a small box of flowers. I stopped. My heart and belly swooped in some synchronised diving routine while my brain held up a scorecard of ten.

"Oh my god," I mumbled, rushing to my door. I put my

grocery bags down and picked up the flowers. They were stunning. "There's a card," I said, though I already knew who they were from. I read the card out loud. "Amaryllis, for last night."

"What's Amaryllis?" Cory asked.

"Must be the type of flower. He's telling me something."

Cory groaned beside me. "Oh god, the standard is high."

I held the flowers to my chest and melted against my door. "The standard is in the stratosphere."

He rolled his eyes. "Open your door."

Oh, right.

I got the door open and carried everything in. Cory unpacked the cold things and put them in the fridge while I googled the floriography of Amaryllis. "Incredibly beautiful," I said.

"What is?"

"The flowers. That's what they mean."

"Oh boy," Cory said flatly. "Yeah, okay, he wins."

I laughed. "The flowers mean *incredibly beautiful*, and he said they were for last night."

My heart was thumping like crazy, and I didn't know if I wanted to laugh or cry. I took out my phone and considered texting but called instead.

He answered on the second ring. "Hello," he said, his voice low and with the hint of a smile.

"I got the flowers. I just got home, and oh my god, Keats. Amaryllis."

"Do you know what they mean?"

"I googled it."

He sighed. "I can't stop thinking about you, about last night."

I could recall so clearly when he'd left. He hadn't wanted to go and had to make himself walk out my door.

I put my hand to my heart and swooned. Actually fucking

swooned, and Cory rolled his eyes and groaned. "I heard about the magic dick," Cory said, loud enough so Keats could hear.

I gasped and shoved him. "Shush."

There was a pause, then Keats said, "Uh, who is that?"

"Cory. We just went grocery shopping, where he managed to only scare three people, so that's like a record. And then he was with me when I found the flowers."

"And he squealed like a girl," Cory yelled.

"I did not," I said.

"And you told him about the . . . what was it? Magic dick?"

I snorted. "I absolutely did, yes. You better believe it. It deserves to be celebrated. Well, bragged about, anyway."

Keats kind of laughed. "Right."

"I would only tell Cory," I amended. "No one else. We share our sex stories. Believe me, I know more about Cory's sex life than I ever really needed to know."

"Bitch, you beg me for details," Cory said flatly.

Keats laughed for real then. "Well, I'm glad there was bragging. Better than embarrassing stories, I guess."

"So much bragging," I said. "Anyway, I just wanted to call you to say thank you for the flowers. They are incredibly beautiful."

He hummed. "So are you. And so was last night."

My dick was now listening. I groaned. "Did you want to come over later? I have to go to Cory's for a few hours, but I'll be home by five."

"I would like that very much," he murmured; the tone of his voice rumbled from my ear straight to my balls. "I'll bring dinner."

"Okay," I whispered, smiling like an idiot.

The line went dead in my ear, and I put my phone to my heart, trying to get my breathing under control.

Cory nodded slowly. "Yeah, okay. I definitely need to meet him. Sooner the better by the look of it."

I MADE IT HOME BY HALF FOUR. JUST ENOUGH TIME to take a shower and watch the clock until there was a knock at my door.

Being busy at Cory's had been fine, but the anticipation of seeing Keats again set my blood abuzz. Not even the prospect of sex or kissing, but just to see him. Yeah, okay, sex too. Because I'd had a semi since my phone call with him.

Yep, I was an absolute goner.

I opened my door, my heart in my throat, unable to stop the grin when I saw him. He held a takeout bag in one hand and something small and pink in his other hand. "Hi," he said, his grin almost as wide as mine.

"Oh god, get in here," I said, all but pulling him in by his shirt. "I've been on edge since you said you were coming over. My dick won't quit."

He laughed and put the bag of food on the kitchen counter. "We can't have that," he said, shoving me up against the countertop, his hand snaking around my jaw, and he crushed his mouth to mine.

It was a filthy kiss.

Intruding tongues, sucking and sliding, and pinning me against the counter with his hips. He made my body sing in ways no one else ever had. I'd never known passion like this. So hot, so consuming.

I could have died right there.

What a fucking way to go.

He broke the kiss, a need for air, apparently. He kept his forehead to mine, his breaths ragged. "I can feel how turned on you are right now," he mumbled, rubbing his erection against mine. "I'm torn. Do I take you to bed right now? Or do I go to my knees for you first?"

Oh god.

My legs almost buckled and my dick throbbed. "Both?" I tried to say.

His smile was slow spreading, his lips still swollen from that kiss. He kissed me again but this time he undid the button on my jeans. "Both, it is."

Then he sank to his knees, right there in my kitchen. He kept me pinned to the kitchen counter, undid the zip, and pulled my cock out. He looked up at me as he closed his lips around me and sucked.

"Oh fuck," I panted. "Fuck, yes."

He worked his tongue, sucking and stroking the shaft, then he hummed around me and I had to think about anything else to stop from coming so soon.

Anything else. Think of anything else.

Then he did some tongue-flicking-while-sucking thing, and there was no way I could hold back.

"God, Keats," I said. "You're gonna make me come so fast."

He groaned around me, then pulled one thigh over his shoulder, gripped my arse, and took me all the way into his throat, and he swallowed.

I saw stars.

Literal fucking stars.

I fisted his hair and shot my load down his throat, with no clue of the unholy sounds I made or what I said.

I could barely stand, and if he hadn't had hold of my leg, if he wasn't holding me against the counter, I would have slithered to the floor.

He let me go and stood up, wrapping his arms around me, now holding me up. He nuzzled his face into my neck. "Mm, you taste delicious."

I barked out a laugh, pretty sure I'd fallen into some nonsensical world where nothing was real. "Jesus," I mumbled.

He chuckled, then pulled back a little and scanned my eyes. "You okay in there?"

"I'm sorry. You've reached the number of Linden Acres. He can't come to the phone right now. Please leave your name and number after the beep and he'll get back to you as soon as he can."

Keats laughed, then cupped my face in both hands. "Hello," he said, still smiling. "I didn't really greet you properly at the door."

"Are you kidding? That was the best hello ever."

He laughed again and softly kissed the tip of my nose. "Oh, I brought you this," he said, taking a pink flower off the countertop. "I made it for you. The flowers were nice, yes, but you like the paper ones."

"Oh." I took the folded pink flower. "It's beautiful. What is it?"

"It's a mezereon," he replied.

"What does it mean?"

He smiled, his eyes meeting mine. "A desire to please."

I snorted. "Well, you nailed that."

He chuckled, warm and lovely.

"But the real flowers were enough. You didn't have to make me this as well."

"Real flowers I can get you anytime. Any kind, any day of the week. They just don't feel special." He touched the paper flower in my hand. "But this? This is from me. I made it just for you."

"One of a kind," I murmured. "Like you."

He gave me a smile that sent my stomach into a somersault.

"And dinner," he said, taking the bag. "I got a mix of Japanese stuff. I wasn't sure what you preferred."

My god, he was just so considerate. My ex wouldn't have even thought to bring dinner at all, let alone consider what I liked and opted to order an array of different things. "I like all of it."

Every single thing.

We sat on my couch and shared every dish, taking bites and smiling, laughing.

"Sprout and Rapunzel seem to like it here," he said, nodding to the two new plants.

"And Leonardo," I added. "I love having them. They brighten my mood. How're Elizabeth and Sebastian?"

"No complaints yet. I have them by the window to the veranda," he said. "And yes, it does brighten the place up. Though it really does reinforce my need to decorate."

"Is it dire?"

"The utmost."

"I'd love to help. Maybe next weekend we could go to IKEA." I stopped, tacking on a very quick, "If you're not busy, that is. Or if you even want to."

I didn't mean to just invite myself . . .

"I'd like that." He smiled, blushing almost. Then he stabbed at some rice with his fork, and I knew he was trying to decide how he should phrase something. Or if he should say something at all. "So you, uh, you told your friend about me?"

I almost laughed with relief. There I was thinking he was going to drop something bad.

"I told Cory about you after the first time I met you and you helped me pick out some flowers that wouldn't kill someone. Though Cory was disappointed my ex wasn't about to meet his karma, he did agree that it was probably for the best. I'm not cut out for prison. Anyway, I said the florist guy was gorgeous and he had a name straight out of a Jane Austen novel and that I had your card, but I was too scared to call you."

His eyebrows shot up. "You were?"

"Yes! Absolutely. You were charming and funny, and you told me I deserved better."

"Because you did," he said, pushing the takeout container onto the coffee table and giving me his undivided attention. "You deserved so much better than that wankstain."

I snorted at that. "And then I told him today that I'd had the best sex of my life last night with this new Mr Wonderful with the perfect name and the perfect dick."

He laughed. "The best?"

"Uncontested. Not only is no one on the same page as you, they're not even in the same book. You, Keats McCulloch, are in a different language, in a different library, on a different planet. That is how far apart you stand."

He chuckled. "Well, I'm flattered. And I'm even a little sorry no one ever did you the way you should have been done. And I say only a little sorry because, while you do deserve to be thoroughly and conclusively had, I'm also a little glad no one's done that to you but me." His smirk drew down on one side. "And I'm also worried now, because the precedent has been set and, with it, a standard I may not live up to. Certainly not every time, and maybe never again."

Laughing, I climbed over and straddled him. He leaned against the backrest of the sofa, his face tilted up to me, and I kissed him softly. "I don't expect it every time, but that doesn't mean we can't try," I murmured, kissing his jaw up to his ear. "Every time."

His hands went straight to my arse and he pulled me closer, lifting his hips up to meet me in a slow grind. I rocked on him, ghosting my lips over his again before settling in for a slow, deep kiss.

I couldn't get enough. My whole body felt electric, desired.

This high, this rush.

This man.

He broke the kiss. "Linden," he said, breathless, his voice strained. "You're killing me here."

I could feel how hard he was, and I rocked on him for good measure. "So take me to bed and do whatever you want to me."

CHAPTER SEVEN
KEATS

I WAS SURE HE WAS OUT TO KILL ME.

Not with murder flowers but with his body. The way he kissed me and rubbed himself against me.

My dick had been ready for action since I dropped to my knees and blew him in his kitchen. Ready at the stop light, engines rumbling, waiting for a green light.

Him climbing onto my lap and melting his body against mine, his hands in my hair, his tongue in my mouth, was about all the torture I could take.

Then he asked me to take him to bed.

I certainly didn't need telling twice. I stood up, holding his arse, and carried him to his room, threw him on the bed, and settled between his thighs.

He laughed, pulling at my shirt and trying to undo my jeans.

It was a scramble to get us both undressed and I kept trying to convince myself to slow down, but my body wouldn't listen.

Neither would my heart.

This was all happening so fast. I was falling in love with

him and that should have scared me, but as I finally pushed into his body, sinking all the way, it was too late.

I wasn't just falling in love with him. I'd already fallen.

And as he clung to me, the way he gasped and whined and arched his back . . . and the way he looked at me—his eyes full of pleading and wonder—I was certain he felt the same.

The way he breathed my name as I slid in and out, driving up into him. The way his legs hooked around my back so he could take all of me.

The way he held my face and pulled my mouth to his when I came. The way he groaned into my mouth and shuddered beneath me as I filled the condom inside him.

Yeah.

I'd already fallen. All the way down.

He filled every corner of my mind. His smile, his smell, his laughter. Even when I was driving to the flower market at five o'clock the next morning, on far less sleep than I was used to. When I arrived back at the shop and unloaded my van with Robbie and Lina.

All I could think about was him.

Robbie put a coffee in my hand and gave me an odd look as he carried a box inside, and later he snapped his fingers at me.

"Oh my god," he said.

I shook my head of all things Linden to find Robbie and Lina both staring at me. I was sitting at the service counter where I was supposed to be processing the day's orders. I must have zoned out.

"Jesus," Robbie said. "You do have it bad."

I groaned out a laugh. I didn't care that my face went red, I didn't care that this was far too premature, and I didn't care that they both knew. "I do. I can't help it. He's . . ." I shook my head. "He's so great."

Robbie pursed his lips and gave me an up and down. "What time did he leave your place last night? You look tired, but you have that sex glow I've never seen on you."

Lina whacked him. "That's not a sex glow. That's an I'm-in-love glow."

I buried my face in my hands. "You're both right?" God, this was embarrassing. "But he didn't leave my place. I left his. At eleven last night."

Lina did a little happy jump. "Eeee! I'm so happy for you!"

Robbie was still staring. "You're in love with him? Already? It's been three weeks."

"I know," I said, agreeing with what he was implying. "I know! It's too much, too soon. We're going to crash and burn because this can't be sustainable, but oh my god, he's . . . he's . . ." I sighed, still smiling. "Perfect."

"There is no such thing as too soon," Lina said. "When the heart knows, the heart knows."

I nodded, but I couldn't ignore Robbie's scepticism. From one gay guy to another. "You've never fallen in love the second you saw someone?"

"Every Friday night," he replied. "But that's not love. That's lust and drugs."

I rolled my eyes. "You love Tan."

"I was coerced into that," he said, sniffing the air. "Consider it Stockholm syndrome-ish, and I'm the victim here. He cast a magic spell on me or something."

I snorted. "Yeah. I remember."

Robbie had technically refused Tan's advances at first, and he'd tried to act indifferent, but theirs was a clear case of Tan fell first, Robbie fell harder because Robbie was so in love with Tan it was ridiculous. Even now, he *still* dotes on him, gives him every single thing he wants, and is fiercely protective of him.

"And how's that working out for you now?" I asked.

He pointed a long stem gerbera at me. "Shush."

Lina was still bouncing. "When are you seeing him again?"

"I don't know," I admitted. "Wednesday, maybe? Definitely on the weekend but I don't know if I can wait that long."

Lina made a high-pitched keening sound, and Robbie sighed. "So, the new outfits worked. You're welcome."

"Yes, he noted the brands, so thank you for that. And he said you had good style."

Robbie arched one eyebrow and pursed his thick lips. "Well, good to know he knows talent when he sees it."

I sighed happily. It felt so bizarre to talk about this so openly. I felt like a giddy schoolboy with a crush.

Remembering how I'd left his place last night, how I'd left him in bed, completely sated. I'd kissed him and made it to his bedroom door before I had to turn around and go back to kiss him again.

I hadn't wanted to leave at all.

It was only the fact I had a 4:30 am alarm that made me leave.

I could still see the smile on his face in the darkened room. His body in a tangle of sheets, too boneless to move, too sleepy. Too beautiful.

I wanted that sight tattooed in my memory.

"I need to send him more flowers," I said. I wanted him to know I was thinking of him. That I hadn't stopped thinking about him.

"Okay, simmer down, lover boy," Robbie said. "Or you'll scare him off."

"Red roses," Lina said. "Classic, stylish."

Robbie made a face. "Cliché." He plucked a white hyacinth out of its bucket. "Loveliness."

Hmm, loveliness.

He sure is that.

"Okay," I agreed. "Perfect."

"How many?" he asked. "The entire bucket full?"

"No, just one." Then I thought about it. "No, maybe I should make him a paper one. It means more. I'll need to google that."

Robbie slow blinked at me, then he speared the hyacinth back into its bucket. "You are a lost cause, my friend. Now hurry up and give us the order list or we may as well shut the shop and go home." He snapped his fingers again. "So look alive. Yes, it's wonderful that you've found love and are finally having sex after the longest drought in gay history, but people are waiting on flower deliveries."

I was just about to tell him to shut up when the door opened, the bell chiming. Lina took her job sheet with a smile and Robbie snatched his with his usual sass, and I greeted the customer.

"Morning," I said, cheerfully.

The said customer was a young guy, maybe early twenties. He wore black-and-white chequered pants, black boots, with a bright orange coat. His hair was styled up, he wore a long silver earring in each ear and bright nail polish.

He turned, his gaze going from my face to my name tag to my face again, and he smiled. "Morning. I'm just looking right now, but I was wondering if you could help me."

I shrugged. "Sure. What can I help you with?"

"I'm after something that sends a message."

Okay then.

"Well, flowers certainly do that. What kind of message? Gratitude, sympathy, congratulations? A *Godfather* style message instead of a horse's head in their bed?"

He smiled. "No, but I like the way you think." He scanned

the display and sighed. "Is there a type of flower that says *I'm trying to decide if you're worthy?*"

I blinked and thought about it. "Well, no one's ever asked me that before. But sure, I mean there would have to be." I gestured to one display. "The pulsatilla means *you have no claim*. Or the white chrysanthemum means *truth* or *honesty*, but you'd need to probably pair it with a butterfly weed, which basically means *consider yourself warned* to really bring home the message. And maybe some coltsfoot. It means *justice will be done to you*. You know, like a bouquet that says *be honest or else*."

He smiled. "I like it."

"Are you thinking full bouquet? Because sometimes a single arrangement has more meaning."

Lina appeared with a printout. She handed it to me. "The origami flower design you wanted," she said.

The customer looked at the piece of paper before I could fold it and put it in my apron pocket.

He tilted his head. "You do folded-paper flowers?" Then he looked around the display room. "I didn't realise that was a thing."

"Oh, it's just for him," Lina said. Then she did a swoon, worthy of an Oscar. "He's in love."

Oh god.

"Ah, thank you," I said to her, giving her a hard glare.

She didn't take the hint to shut up. "After all, what does one give to show his love when he could give any flower in the world?"

I sighed again. "Yes, thanks, Lina."

Then she looked at the customer and nodded to his hand, to his nail polish. "This colour is fabulous."

He grinned and held his fingers out. "Thank you. It's Atomic Tangerine."

Then Robbie came in, holding the store phone out for me. "Sorry, boss. It's Linden. He said it's urgent. He tried your mobile twice, but it rang out."

I felt my back pocket, then realised I'd left my phone on the service desk. But Linden? Calling me and saying it's urgent?

"I'm sorry, I must take this call," I said to the customer, gesturing for Robbie and Lina to please take care of him. I put the phone to my ear and took a step back. "Hello? Linden, is everything okay? What's wrong?"

"Oh my god," he said, pure relief. "Okay, look. You're about to get a customer. He's short, has black hair, probably wearing something baby-girl punkish, has orange nail polish—"

I turned to face the customer. He wasn't paying any attention to Lina or Robbie. He was smiling at me.

"Ah, he's here now," I said slowly.

Linden groaned. "I'm going to kill him." But then he sighed. "That is my soon-to-be ex-best friend Cory. Can you please put him on the phone? I'll explain everything, I just need to yell at him first."

I held the phone out for him. "He wants to speak to you."

He laughed, and Lina and Robbie both shot me a confused look, and Cory stood there, grinning like the Cheshire Cat. "Hello," he purred into the phone. "Oh, Linden, baby, don't be like that. . . . Yes, I know. . . . I told you I wanted to meet him without you so I could see what he's like when you're not around, and I have to say," he said smoothly, still smiling at me. "He's quite charming. And hot."

Oh god.

Robbie looked at me. "Do you know this guy?"

"I think it's Linden's best friend." Then I remembered

what kind of flowers he'd asked for. "Doing a spy-check on me to see if I'm worthy."

Robbie clucked his tongue. "Oh, I like them already." Then he swished his way to the back door. "I'll be getting my work done, like nobody else here today, apparently."

Lina took that as her cue. "I'll leave you to it," she said, smiling as she followed Robbie into the back room.

"Oh sweetie," Cory said into the phone. "That's some mighty colourful language. . . . Yes, okay. I'm sorry. . . . Because I'm not sorry, sorry . . ." He sighed and rolled his eyes then handed me back the phone. "He wants to talk to you."

I took the phone, trying not to smile. "Hello?"

"My god, Keats. I'm so sorry."

"Don't apologise. You have nothing to be sorry for. Neither does Cory. It's fine. It's kinda sweet, actually."

"Can you not say that to him, please," Linden said. "Be mad at him. Like I am."

I chuckled. "It's fine, honestly. Are you outside somewhere?" It sounded like he was near traffic.

"Yes, I'm in line at Hermès. I have an appointment, which they're late for. It's why I couldn't run down to your shop and kill Cory in person."

"Oh, an appointment? Is everything okay?" I wasn't sure who or what Hermès was.

He chuckled. "Yes, it's a store."

A store. "And you have an appointment? For a store?"

"Yes. You know how they have lines of people waiting outside the ultra-exclusive retail stores?"

I didn't know that. "Uh, sure?"

"You need to make an appointment to buy a ten-thousand-dollar Birkin handbag from Hermès and still have to wait outside for an hour, and I can tell you my clients won't be doing that. They pay me to hold the appointment and make the purchase on their behalf."

"Ten thousand dollars for a handbag?"

He laughed quietly. "Oh, yes. That's nothing. Anyway, I won't keep you. Please tell Cory he's in so much trouble and that I'll deal with him later."

"I will."

"And you can ignore the frantic voicemails I left on your phone."

I grinned. "I will."

"Ooh, I'm being let in. Gotta go."

The line went dead in my ear, so I slid my phone into my apron pocket and smiled at Cory, holding out my hand. "Keats. Nice to meet you."

His grin widened as he shook my hand. "Cory. No hard feelings, I hope."

"None."

"I had to meet you, and I wanted it to be when he wasn't around so I could see the real you and not you on your best behaviour in front of him."

I nodded. "I can appreciate that." Then I held my breath. "And did I pass?"

He narrowed his eyes. "So far. The *Godfather* reference was a strong start." He scrutinised me for a long moment. "And you're making him another paper flower?"

"I am. Well, I was going to." I cleared my throat. "It probably seems childish, but it means more than anything I could give him from my shop. And he seems to like them."

"He loves them. Because it does mean more than anything you could give him from here." He looked around at the displays. "So I suppose you pass, though the test is ongoing."

"I would hope it to be so," I replied with a smile.

He smirked at me, and although he tried to be a hard-arse, I knew he liked me.

"Just so you know," he added. "Linden has had terrible luck with men. He's too nice, too forgiving, and he often gets walked all over because of that." He put his hand to his chest. "I am neither nice nor forgiving."

I tried to stop from smiling. "Message received and understood."

He nodded. "Glad we understand each other." Then he gave me a blinding smile and looked at the display of flowers we were standing in front of. "Just out of curiosity, if I wanted to perhaps give someone a flower that said I was interested—" He put his hand up. "But not too interested—because one must act aloof—which would you suggest?"

I could tell why he and Linden were friends. I'd known Cory for all of two minutes and I already liked him. I took a second to think about his question and looked around to see what I had in store. "Well, the viscaria is a bold choice. It means *join me in this dance*. Not just an actual dance, but the dance of romance, or the dance of whatever you have going on."

"Is there a flower that says *I'm just here for the dick*?"

I barked out a laugh, grateful no one else was in the store. "Uh, not that I know of."

He frowned as he hummed. "I don't know if he's a flower type of guy. He's a big, tough bad guy." He rolled his eyes. "Except he's not really. He's a huge teddy bear. But if I were to give him flowers on a date or something, I think he'd be embarrassed."

I nodded. "What if you were to wear one flower on your lapel?" I plucked one long-stemmed jonquil from a bucket and held it to his jacket collar. "Probably not with this orange jacket, but it could look sweet with a darker colour. And this flower means *please return my affection* but that could imply *please return my affection for dick*. So, if he mentions the flower, you can bring it up."

Cory smiled. "I like that."

I handed the flower to him. "Take it. Use it, and I hope you get what you're after."

He laughed. "So do I." He walked to the door and stopped. "I shall report back in with Linden and say you passed the first test."

I nodded seriously, though I had to fight a smile. "I shall do the same."

With a smirk, he disappeared out the door. I found my phone and listened to Linden's voicemails with a ridiculously stupid grin on my face. I knew he was busy so I shot him a text in response.

> Cory said I passed the first test.

Then I shoved my phone into my pocket and got to work, but I checked my phone during my lunch break to see he'd replied.

> He told me you were sweet and charming. I'm sorry he bombarded you at work. Call you later tonight?

I thumbed out a quick reply.

> I'd like that

Then, not long after Cory had left, I had another visitor at work. This time it was a woman in a sharp pant suit and long brown hair. She had a satchel tucked under her arm and a professional smile. She looked around my showroom as if she was assessing something.

I approached her like I would any customer. "Hi! How can I help you?"

"Yes," she said smoothly. "My name's Megan Morano. I believe you did a job for Linden Acres. Some red orchids and a kumquat tree."

Ah, right.

The real estate agent who wanted my card.

"Yes!" I replied. "I certainly did. My name's Keats."

"Well, I loved your work, Keats. And your efficiency. Would you be interested in regular work? I can't guarantee frequency, perhaps one or two jobs per week, maybe less. Maybe more. But most jobs will be short notice. It's a fast-paced industry and that's the nature of the beast, I'm afraid."

"I'd be very interested. However, some requests will depend on seasonal availability, and where I can source them from. That's the nature of this beast."

She didn't seem concerned. "I'll be leaving the specific requests to Linden. He's the one who knows what the client needs. His business reflects on mine, so I just wanted to drop in and meet you."

I tried not to smile too hard. "That's fine with me. I'll discuss options with Linden directly then, yes?"

"By all means. Though Linden doesn't do all my listings, so if I decide I need something else, I can contact you directly."

"Absolutely." I handed her my card.

She took the business card and held out her hand for me to shake. "I'll be in touch."

She left and I stood there, letting out a low breath.

"Who was that?" Robbie asked, coming over to stand beside me.

"That could be a pretty decent work contract."

Robbie clapped my shoulder. "Love to see it."

MY PHONE RANG A BIT AFTER SEVEN AND LINDEN'S name on my screen made my heart beat double time.

"Hello," I said.

"Hey," he replied. "Oh my god, I'm so sorry Cory came to see you at work."

I snorted. "Don't apologise, it's fine. I'm actually kinda glad he did. It's out of the way now, and I don't have to be a nervous wreck for a week leading up to some planned meeting."

He laughed quietly. "This is true. I had no idea he was going to see you until he called me when he was almost there. I think he wanted to torture me, as he does. I did try to warn you."

"You did. Your second voicemail was my favourite. The stricken panic, the urgency. The anger directed at Cory."

He gasped. "Please tell me you deleted them."

I chuckled. "I haven't yet. But I will if you want me to."

"Yes, please."

"Okay. Oh, and I had another visitor at work today."

"Oh?"

"Megan Morano. She came in to introduce herself. Said I could be working with you in the future or for other listings that aren't yours."

"Eek! Is that a good thing?"

"Very good. I get to work with you, and the possibility of steady contracts. That's amazing! I should thank you."

He hummed, all sexy. "You can. Anytime."

I groaned. "Not helping."

He let out a sigh. "What are you doing right now?"

"I'm on my couch, watching some crap on Netflix I can't even remember the name of, and I'm eating a supermarket salad for dinner. I'm in my sad, single gay era, apparently."

He was quiet for a beat. "Single, huh?"

Oh shit.

"Uh . . . Well, um, technically, yes?"

He sighed. "Well, technically, yes. I guess that's true. Given we haven't discussed anything about expectations or labels . . ."

Holy shit.

We were actually having this conversation . . .

My heart rate was now staccato.

"I mean, we don't have to," he added quickly.

"I'd like to," I said, unsure of how I even managed to speak. "I wasn't really expecting this conversation, but now that we're having it, I think we could talk about expectations. I mean, I'd like to. If you want to?"

He made a happy sound. "I want to."

Oh boy.

He let out a breath, sounding as nervous as me. "Should we do it over the phone? Or should we wait until the next time we see each other?"

"I don't mind. Whichever you'd prefer. I'm happy just knowing you want to talk about it, so at least I know we're on the same page."

"It's crazy fast, isn't it?"

"Yes. But it feels right, don't you think?"

"I do." Then he laughed. "God, this is insane."

I couldn't help but laugh too. Relieved and so freaking happy. "Maybe we could discuss some options now, and when we see each other next, we can say what we're comfortable with. You know, if we take a day or two to think them over."

"Sounds fair."

"Well, I'd be happy to put dating on the table, straight up," I said. "We are technically dating, so that's more of an observation than a label."

"True." It sounded as if he was smiling.

Okay, so we were officially dating. Good to know.

I was nervous. Giddy, almost. "As for expectations," I said. "And this is something you can tell me if you're comfortable with or not. But I definitely won't be seeing anyone else while I'm dating you. I'm a one-person-only kinda guy. But that's just me, and I know that's not cool with everyone. Dating means keeping options open, I guess. So if you wanted to date other people, I'd be okay with that."

"Would you really, Keats?"

"No."

He laughed. "Me either. I don't want to see anyone else. I won't be dating anyone else, and I like the fact you won't be either."

Oh, wow.

"Sooo," he added, "does that mean we're exclusive? You know, as far as expectations and labels go? You don't need to answer that right now—"

"Yes."

He chuckled. "So much for leaving the answers until we see each other next."

"You can answer whenever you're comfortable," I replied. "But I know my answer already."

"I know mine too," he murmured. Then he was quiet again, and I wasn't sure what to say next.

Because what came next was a big step.

"Sooo," he said again. "Exclusive dating sounds a lot like boyfriends."

And there it was.

He said it.

My heart felt a little strangled. Nerves and butterflies and something else I was nowhere near ready to name yet.

"It does," I managed to say. "I'm happy to keep it at dating exclusively if that takes any pressure off."

He let out a shaky breath in my ear and it sent a shiver through me.

Hoooooooly shit.

"Boyfriends, huh," he said, as if he was trying how it sounded for size.

"How about you leave your answer until we see each other," I suggested. "Say, Wednesday night? My place?"

"Sounds good." Then he added, "What about your answer?"

"I already know my answer."

He chuckled. "Fucking hell."

I was now grinning like an idiot, my dinner long forgotten. "Unless you wanted to come over tomorrow night . . ."

He barked out a laugh. "You have no idea how much I'd like that. Six o'clock okay?"

"Perfect. We can order in some dinner."

"Deal."

We were both quiet then, but I didn't want to hang up. "I should let you go," I tried.

"Yeah," he breathed but made no attempt to hang up.

"I'll text you my address."

"Okay."

More silence. "Okay look," I said. "I need to go before I ask you to come over tonight. Or before I find myself going to your place."

He laughed. "Yes. Same. Okay, good night, Keats."

"Good night, Linden."

I had to make myself end the call, but I smiled for the rest of the night.

I was still smiling, even when I got to the flower markets early the next morning and all the way into the shop.

Robbie gave me one look, then rolled his eyes. "Oh god. It's getting worse."

I laughed but Lina chided him. "Leave him alone. He's happy."

We unloaded the van and began our workday, and I couldn't remember ever feeling so damn happy.

Then around ten o'clock, my phone rang and *Mum* flashed on the screen. I held it up for Lina to see. "Just be a minute," I said, then walked outside and answered the call. "Hey, Mum."

"Oh hey, love, just thought I'd call you to see how you are."

"Yeah, I'm good," I replied. Not even the grey day outside could ruin my mood. "Everything's good."

"How's the store? Busy as ever?"

"Yep."

There was a beat of silence. "What's wrong? That sounded unfinished."

I laughed. "Nothing's wrong. The opposite, actually."

"Oh?"

I took a deep breath and exhaled. "Maybe I'm jinxing myself here, but I might have met someone."

"Oh, Keats, that's wonderful news. Who is he?"

"Ah, no names yet. Or I will jinx myself. It's only very early days. It's too early to be telling you, probably. Definitely." I was regretting saying anything at all.

"How early?" Mum asked.

"Well, just a few weeks, Mum. A handful of dates."

"You've been single a long time."

"Yeah, thanks for the reminder."

She laughed. "I didn't mean that in a bad way. What I'm saying is just enjoy it, love. It might be so new and exciting because you've been single so long, but that doesn't make it any less real. I'm just glad you're happy."

I sighed, now not regretting telling her so much. "Thanks, Mum."

"So what does he do?"

"No details."

"Where did you meet him? One of those online sex apps, I suppose. It's what young people do these days."

"Oh my god, no, Mum. Please don't." I cringed. "It wasn't an app. He came into my store."

"Ooh, meeting someone the old-fashioned way."

"Okay, Mum, no more details. I don't want to jinx it."

"Well, just let us know when you want to bring him around for dinner—"

Good lord.

"Mum, it's a bit early for that, I think."

We might have used the word boyfriends last night, but that still wasn't officially confirmed, and even then, meeting parents was a whole new level of commitment.

She sighed. "Well, I'm glad you're happy, that's all. I hope it works out."

"Same, Mum. Same. I'm trying not to get too invested." Then I sighed. "I better get back inside. We're busy. Tell Dad I said hi."

"I will. Oh, and don't forget it's your sister's birthday next week."

I'd totally forgotten. "I didn't forget."

"Okay, love. I'm glad I called. Take care."

"Bye, Mum."

I pocketed my phone and went back inside. Robbie was talking to a customer, and I knew he was due for deliveries so I intervened so he could leave.

And I got so busy with work for the rest of the afternoon, I hadn't had a chance to think about anything else until we closed the front door to the shop.

We packed up, cleaned up, and I thanked both Lina and Robbie for being so great, not just today but for always being so great. Lina was all sweet smiles as she dragged Robbie out, because he was looking at me as if I'd sprouted a second head.

Maybe I'd been grumpier than I'd realised these last few years.

Maybe my now-permanent smile scared him. Maybe me whistling along to the music playlist was a bit much today.

I couldn't even bring myself to care.

And six o'clock couldn't come around fast enough. I finished some accounts at work, put in more stock orders before I shut everything down and locked up. I picked up some pasta and garlic bread on the way home for dinner, even grabbed a bottle of wine.

Yep.

So much for not getting too invested. I was well and truly in over my head.

I was fixing my hair in the mirror and telling myself not to get too carried away at ten to six when there was a knock on my door. A quick glance through the peephole showed me a nervous-smiling Linden and I pulled the door open.

"Hey."

He sighed when he saw me, then threw his arms around me, his face in my neck. "Hey," he mumbled.

I managed to shove the door closed, and then I just held him.

For a few seconds, just with our arms around each other. He was on his toes, so I picked him up and gave him a bit of a squeeze before setting him down. He smelled amazing. He felt even better.

"I was trying to play it cool," he said. Then he slid his hand up to my face. "But then I saw you." He leaned up on his tiptoes again, this time so he could kiss me. A soft, slow press of his lips.

"I've been trying to play it cool too," I admitted. Then I pinched his chin between my thumb and forefinger. I scanned his eyes, then took in every detail of his face. "Christ, look at you," I mumbled before kissing him again. Deeper this time, lips parted.

He chuckled. "Something in here smells good."

Oh, right.

I took a step back. "Dinner is warming in the oven," I said. "Come on in."

I showed him my very basic living room, my boring kitchen. "Ooh, Elizabeth is looking happy by the window," he said, lightly touching the leaves. "And Sebastian."

"You can see what I mean about needing a makeover though, right?" I said, gesturing to the couch and old coffee table.

He met my gaze. "This is all fine," he offered. "But yes. Yes, I can."

I laughed. "Oh, before I forget. I made you this."

I took the paper flower and handed it to him.

He sucked back a quiet breath and set the flower in the palm of his hand. "Keats, it's so pretty. You made this one too?"

I nodded. "Google is my friend. Well, actually, Lina found the design and printed it off for me."

He gently touched the petal. "What kind is it?"

"A white hyacinth. It means *loveliness*. Because that's what you are."

His eyes met mine. "It's . . . perfect."

My heart was about to burst out of my chest. The frantic thrumming was making me a little lightheaded.

I needed to change the subject.

"Oh, dinner is a roasted vegetable linguine and garlic bread. I'd like to claim that I made it, but we'd both know I was lying. I got it from Alberto's."

He rubbed his stomach. "Sounds perfect. I'm actually kinda hungry."

But then he stood there and stared, and I stared right back. Not sure how to bring up the boyfriend conversation but desperately wanting to, and I was pretty sure he wanted to mention it too. "If you're hungry, we should eat . . ."

He nodded, and setting the table gave us something to do. There was a definite elephant in the room, but it was an excited, nervous elephant.

When we had the food in the middle of the table and plates set, I held up a wine glass. "I have some pinot noir, if you want one?"

He smiled as he sat. "Sure."

After I dished up some pasta for us both and he poured the wine, it was back to silence. We ate a few bites and he hummed and did a little happy wiggle in his seat.

But the elephant in the room could have very well had a seat at the table.

The silence was becoming awkward . . .

"So," we both said at the same time. Then we both laughed.

"You go first," I said, opting out like the chicken I apparently was.

"Oh," he said, frowning at his pasta. "So the other day we mentioned status and expectations . . ."

Oh boy.

Here it was.

"Yeah," I said lamely. I put my fork down. "Look, I don't want you to feel pressured, or if you think it's too soon—"

"No, I don't," he said quickly. "I mean, it is."

Oh.

I nodded, that acknowledgement cutting a little deeper than I'd expected.

"But it's also not," he amended gently.

When I looked up, his eyes were on me. Soft and kind. Then he smiled. "And if we've already established that we're dating and being exclusive, then I think the term boyfriend can apply."

My breath left me in a whoosh, and I laughed. The butterflies in my belly were now in full flight. "I think it could too."

He chuckled, and the awkwardness between us was gone. "I don't know why that was so hard to say."

I laughed. "Me either! I thought you were going to say no or that it was too soon. Because I think we can both agree that it is." Then I shrugged. "But it's also not."

He smiled when I repeated what he'd said earlier. "I was never saying no. Even if Cory had come back waving a huge red flag, I'd probably still just jump in with both feet."

I was still smiling, so very relieved. "I liked Cory," I said. "I liked that he came to see if I was a giant douche. That means he's looking out for you, and honestly, everyone needs a friend like that."

"Be careful what you wish for, because yes, he's great. He's also a lot. He has a flair for the dramatic. I mean, I love him with my whole entire heart, but some days I could strangle him."

I chuckled. "Do I even want to know what he said about me?"

"He said his first impression of you was good."

"He did tell me that, yes," I said. "Then he kinda departed with a thinly veiled threat that the tests of worthiness would be ongoing."

Linden laughed. "He's such a brat." He sipped his wine. "But he was impressed with you. He said you referenced the *Godfather* movie, so that was a win because he loves those movies." His eyes softened and his smile turned sweet. "And he also said you were making me another paper flower because they mean more than any kind of flower at your store."

"Yeah, I told you that before."

"Yes, but you told *him* that, and he said your cheeks went bright pink and you got all shy and that you'd enlisted the help of the woman that works for you, and so Cory deduced you'd been speaking about me, about the flowers, like it was a big deal." He inhaled deeply. "Cory thought that if you'd been secretive or denied the paper flower thing that it meant you had something to hide, but you didn't."

Okay, wow.

"Both Lina and Robbie know," I said. "Robbie and Tan took me shopping, remember? And Lina helped with the origami flowers. Of course they know. Lina's quite invested, I think. She's very happy for me that I'm finally seeing someone. And Robbie . . ." I made a face. "I think Robbie has concerns about my mental health. Apparently now I'm too happy, which he assumed was the fact I was now having sex."

Linden laughed. "Well, is he wrong?"

"Not entirely." I chuckled. "I am happier. And I don't want you to panic that my happiness is hinged solely on you or our being together. I mean, I am happier because of that, but it was time. I was ready." I took a deep breath in. "I'm just glad I met you when I did."

"I'm glad I met you when I did too." He twirled some pasta onto his fork. "And this is really good. You offering me pasta, wine, and sex makes for a very happy Linden."

I snorted. "I haven't offered you sex tonight."

He chewed his mouthful and washed it down with a sip of wine. "Not yet, but you're gonna." Then he nodded at my plate. "Eat up. You're gonna need the sustenance."

THE REST OF THE WEEK WENT BY IN A FLASH. WORK was busy, and I had an ongoing stream of text conversations with Linden, but Friday couldn't come fast enough.

I was expected at his place by seven. He was ordering dinner and I'd be staying the night. So we could go shopping early on Saturday morning, was his reasoning.

I held absolutely zero objections.

Spending the night, sleeping next to him was a logical next step.

For boyfriends.

I knocked on his door at ten to seven and he opened the door for me with a smile. "Hello, handsome," he said.

"Hey." I stepped inside and he didn't really step aside so I found myself right up against him, so pressing him against the wall and kissing him was a completely logical next step.

For boyfriends.

"Mm," he hummed, smiling. "Hello, handsome, indeed."

It was weird how I'd managed to go months without sex before, and now even having sex once or twice a week wasn't enough. I pinned him against the wall with my hips, letting him feel how turned on I was. What he did to me.

"Oh fuck," he said. "I was gonna ask what takeout you wanted to order, but dinner can wait." He took my hand and led me to his room.

"I can wait if you're hungry," I began.

He turned to face me, his back to the bed, and he pulled me in for a hot, hard kiss. "I'm hungry for you," he murmured, pulling my shirt over my head, then trying for the button on my jeans. "Christ."

I was about to argue, trying to pace this, trying to slow us down, but then he slipped his hand down my briefs and stroked my erection.

And then I couldn't argue.

There was no turning back, no stopping. I couldn't get enough of him, and from the way he was working me over and trying to help me get undressed, it was safe to guess he felt the same.

We fell onto the bed in a mass of limbs and urgent mouths and desperate fingers and whispered pleas. Passion and desire, so fucking hot.

I couldn't get inside him fast enough.

I needed to sink into him, bury myself deep and never return. I wanted to lose myself in his heat, succumb to his every desire and whim.

I couldn't get deep enough. I couldn't get enough.

And as I drove into him, over and over, pulling out to the tip, then sliding back into the hilt. Watching every flicker of pleasure in his eyes, every emotion and tasting it all on his tongue.

The way he held onto me, the way he arched his back when he came, and my god, the way he whispered my name.

His cock pulsed between us, and his seed spurted onto his belly.

I tumbled over the edge right after him. My orgasm set fire to my blood, to my bones, and I came hard. I lost all sight and sound, the room spun, and Linden writhed under me, groaning with me.

I collapsed on top of him, and he laughed. "Holy fuck," he said, breathless.

It took a few moments for my senses to come back to me, his fingers tracing gentle patterns over my back. I wished I could stay inside him forever. I wished I didn't have to move, but of course that wasn't the case.

I slowly pulled out of him and got to my knees, but when I looked down, what I saw stopped me cold.

"Oh shit," I said. "Linden."

He half sat up. "What's wrong? Did you break my arsehole?"

I didn't laugh. I just shook my head and pulled the torn condom off. "No. I broke the condom."

CHAPTER EIGHT
LINDEN

Broken condom.

I heard the words, and logically I knew what that meant.

But it was the look on Keats' face that scared me.

"Oh god, I'm so sorry," he said. "I must have been too rough or too much. I did something wrong. Did I hurt you? Oh god, Linden, did I hurt you?"

He was pale and his eyes were wide, like he was about to have a full-blown panic attack. "No, you didn't hurt me. You, uh," I gestured to the smear of jizz on my belly. "You made me come without touching my dick."

But he really was freaking out, so maybe joking wasn't the right approach.

Broken condom.

I could see the condom. It had torn almost up the entire length of it and his come was leaking out onto his hand. Which meant it was inside me.

And I knew what that meant.

But the look on his face. He was horrified.

"Keats," I tried. "Are you . . . are you . . . ?"

He shook his head. "I'm so sorry."

I grabbed his arm. "Are you . . . are you positive? What's your status?" Oh god. Why hadn't we discussed this before?

His eyes met mine, wide as saucers. "What? Oh god, no. No, I'm negative. I mean, I was in my last test. And there's only been one other time in the last coupla months. It was a random hook-up about three or four months ago, and I wore a condom, of course."

Relief flooded through me. "Okay."

He was now looking at me, waiting . . . "Are you . . . ?"

"I'm negative. I got tested straight after I found out Jason cheated on me."

He sagged back on his haunches, and he let out a breath. "God. I'm still . . . I'm so sorry. I didn't feel it break. I should have. It was just so intense, I . . ."

I sat up properly. "I don't expect you to have known, Keats."

Then I realised . . . what I could feel. "Oh," I said, getting off the bed. "I should probably get cleaned up."

His eyes popped open, and he scrambled off the bed too. "Oh god, yes, shit. Is there something I should do?"

Uh. You could stop panicking. That'd be a great start.

"I'll just have a shower," I said. "Gimme a few minutes."

He nodded quickly. "Yes, of course."

He was standing there as naked as me, with his cock hanging heavy, with his palm out still holding the offending condom in a pool of jizz on his hand.

"Maybe you should get cleaned up too," I suggested.

"Good idea." He turned in each direction, then stopped, unsure.

I almost laughed, and I knew that probably wasn't the right response. Maybe I was having a delayed reaction. He was in panic mode, clearly. While I felt . . . decidedly calm. I took his wrist and pulled him toward my bathroom. "Come with me."

I wrapped the condom in a wad of toilet paper and tossed it into the bin and turned the shower on, and that seemed to kick-start Keats into gear. Because gone was the floundering guy who didn't know what to do, and in his place was someone who was focused.

He was focused on me.

He scrubbed us both down with the soapy loofah, but then he took his time gently washing me. It was with a sense of reverence, almost. He was quiet, serious, and clearly very sorry.

Then he cupped my face and pressed a soft kiss to my lips. "I'll give you a minute, okay?"

I gave a nod, and he got out, wrapped a towel around himself, and left me alone.

His reaction was a little weird. Granted, this whole scenario was unexpected and not ideal, but I was getting a glimpse of Keats that I hadn't seen.

And that was the crux of it. Because yes, we'd gone and fallen headfirst into a relationship, boyfriend territory, and yet we didn't know each other. Not really.

Not at all.

I took some time to clean my arse, which Keats had done too, and for all the good intentions, it made no difference. The damage was done.

If there was damage done, that was.

I guess finding that out was the next step.

I shut off the water, dried off, and got dressed. I noticed Keats' clothes were gone from my bedroom floor and I had to wonder if he was even still here . . .

The house was quiet and I had a godawful feeling that he'd bailed.

But when I walked out to my living room, he was there on

the couch, looking at his phone. He stood up when he saw me. "Hey," he said gently. "How are you feeling?"

"I'm fine," I replied.

Because I was.

He held up his phone. "There's a twenty-four-hour health clinic in Surry Hills." Then he swallowed hard. "If you want me to take you. I'll understand if you'd rather not."

"If I'd rather not?"

His nostrils flared and he—god, was he about to cry?

"I'm sorry. I didn't mean for this to happen, and you can be mad at me. Or blame me, I—"

"Okay, stop," I said, walking to him and taking his hand. "It's not your fault. I don't blame you."

"You don't?"

I shook my head. "No. Not at all. Let's just deal with it."

He nodded. "Okay. I'm sorry I freaked out before."

"You're still kinda freaking out."

"I know. I'm sorry, I just . . . I feel responsible."

I took a deep breath in. "I'm going to call Cory. He's more adept at this stuff."

He opened his mouth, then promptly shut it and nodded. "Okay, yes. Whatever you need."

I took my phone and dialled Cory's number. He answered on the fourth ring. "This better be good," he said. "You're interrupting a very good thing right now."

"Uh, we just had a condom break," I said. "We're heading to the clinic on Crown Street."

I looked at Keats and he nodded quickly.

There was a brief pause on the phone, then the sound of muffled movement. I could hear Cory say something to some-one, then he spoke to me. "I'll meet you there."

THE CLINIC WAS TUCKED IN A LONG, NARROW building. There was a small waiting room at the front with the service desk, a long hall down the right-hand side with examination rooms off it. When we walked in, Keats kept his hand on the small of my back and he gave our details, and we sat down in the waiting room to fill in our paperwork. When that was done, Keats handed our clipboards back and fell back into the seat beside me.

"You okay?" he asked.

"Sure. You?"

He shrugged. "I thought when you said you'd call Cory, it meant you didn't want me to come with you." His expression was sad, worried.

I patted his leg. "I thought you looked a bit dejected."

He let out a sigh. "You're taking this way better than me."

Before I could reply, the door opened and Cory burst through. He wore his black skinny jeans and a purple T-shirt, and he sagged when he saw us. Then a man came in behind him. Tall, dark, and handsome, and somewhat familiar.

"Okay, my raw-dogging kings," Cory said. "Don't panic, I'm here."

"Oh god," Keats said, slumping back in his seat.

"I don't think someone's at the joking stage just yet," I said, giving Cory a pointed look.

He looked at Keats and winced. "Sorry."

I then looked to the guy with Cory. He was standing back a little. "Hi. Sorry, don't mind Cory's lack of manners. I'm Linden, and this is Keats."

He gave a nod. "Amon."

"Ah, I did meet you once before," I said. "At whichever club that was. Sorry for interrupting your night."

Cory hooked his arm through Amon's and led him to a spare seat. "You did interrupt," Cory said. "Though we clearly weren't having as much fun as you two. Tell me what happened?"

"Condom broke," I said. "Not much more to explain than that."

"Full- or mid-use?"

Keats groaned, but I answered. "Full."

"And sexual histories were discussed, right?" Cory pressed. "Your statuses were disclosed prior to any of this, right?"

There was a beat of silence before a woman with a clipboard came out. "Keats and Linden?" she asked. "Together or separate appointments?"

"Together," I said, taking Keats' hand and standing up.

May as well get it over and done with.

She led us down the hall to one open door and waited for us both to walk in. We sat and relayed what had happened.

"Sexual history since your last screening?" she asked, looking at me first.

"I was tested over a month ago. No one but Keats since then."

Then she looked at Keats.

"Ah, my last check-up was about four months ago. I had one random hook-up about three months ago?" He gave me an apologetic grimace. "No one since Linden."

"And you wore protection?"

"Yes."

The woman smiled. "Which of you bottomed?"

I put my hand up, and Keats sighed.

He really wasn't taking this whole thing well. I slid my hand into his and his grip was immediately tight.

"Are you on PrEP or any—"

I shook my head. "No."

"And how long have you two been having sex?"

"Uh, two weeks?" I answered, looking at Keats.

He nodded. "Yeah."

"No other sexual partners in this time?"

We both shook our heads. "No," I replied. "We're exclusive," I said, trying to smile for Keats.

His returning smile fell flat.

She gave me a sympathetic nod. "Baptism of fire, huh?"

"Yeah, apparently."

"Okay, let's start with you, Linden."

Swabs, samples, and bloods taken, then it was Keats' turn. He was polite and accommodating to the clinician, not that I expected him not to be. But he was standoffish with me.

No, not standoffish.

Scared?

I wasn't sure.

He was different.

When we were done with the blood tests, the clinician looked at the HIV rapid tests and gave us a reassuring smile. "Immediate screenings are negative," she said. "For both of you."

I sighed with relief, and Keats pressed the heel of his hand to his stomach and let out a huge breath. "Thank you."

She explained that while it was a good indication of our prior status, it was perhaps too early to detect anything from tonight. But if one of us was positive prior, at least we'd know. She reminded us, any rapid results weren't a conclusive finding, and we wouldn't know full results until all swab and blood test results were in. That could take a while.

I nodded, because I knew this. "Yes, thank you."

But she eyed Keats. "Are you okay?"

He nodded quickly, then swallowed hard. "I just, uh . . ." He let out a rush of breath. "Positives can take a few months to show up, right? And I had that random hook-up three months ago, so if my results come back positive, could that mean I infected Linden? Because god—"

He was about to freak out, so I took his hand and squeezed. "Hey. My ex also cheated on me, remember?"

The clinician studied us both but spoke to Keats first. "You said you used protection with the random hook-up three months ago."

He nodded again. "Yes. I did. Of course."

Then she turned to me. "Did you use condoms with your ex?"

"Yes. Which he insisted on, which makes sense in hindsight. At least he did one thing right." I shrugged. "I've never had unprotected sex before. And all my results came back negative."

She gave us a smile. "Okay, so we've both taken the right steps." She patted Keats arm. "It's perfectly natural to feel responsible, but accidents happen."

"He's not responsible," I said. I looked at Keats and gave his hand a shake so he'd look at me. "Hey. I told you before, it's not your fault."

He winced again. "I know, I just . . ." He sighed. "I feel like I came inside you without your consent, and honestly, it makes me feel sick."

Oh boy.

"Keats," I whispered.

"Doing anything without your consent, without your permission . . ." He shook his head and pressed his hand against his stomach again.

"Okay, you know what?" I said. "I think we should discuss this at home."

He nodded and swallowed hard.

I gave the nurse a pointed look. "Please tell him it was not his fault."

Her smile at him was fond, sympathetic. "It was not your fault. You didn't do this deliberately, did you?"

His gaze shot to hers, wild. "What? No!"

She shrugged. "Then you are not to blame. Condoms break. It doesn't happen often, but it does happen. Though it's not necessary, but might I suggest getting condoms in a larger size?"

"Oh god," Keats mumbled, his face red.

I almost laughed. I mean, she had seen his dick when she swabbed him. "And we'll be throwing out the remainder from the box of the faulty one."

"Good idea." The nurse gave Keats a smile. "You're not to blame, okay?"

He relented a nod and I squeezed his hand.

The nurse straightened the paperwork. "Should we discuss the need for PrEP or anything else while you're here?"

"Oh." I wasn't sure . . . Keats looked at me for an answer, but I resisted sighing. "How about we just deal with this first? We'll go home and have a chat about it."

She smiled, nodding. "Sure."

"Okay then," I said. "Are we done?"

She gave a nod and wrapped up the appointment with the reiteration that positive results don't mean the end of the world, and how there were now many options for living a full, healthy life should we need to cross that bridge when we get to it.

"Yes, understood. Thank you," I said, standing up.

Keats did the same. "Thank you so much."

He rushed to open the door for me and got to the hall. He paused and pointed his thumb at the bathroom door. "I need to pee."

"Sure. Of course. I'll be in the waiting room."

I found Cory and Amon still waiting.

Cory noticed I was on my own. His expression drew grim. "Is everything okay? Where's Keats?"

I sat next to him. "He's just using the bathroom."

His brow furrowed. "Is he . . . is everything okay?"

I sighed. "Prelim results all negative, but . . ."

"But what?"

"I dunno, Core. He's been weird. I don't know if he just doesn't handle this stuff too well, but he freaked out at home. Got all panicky and worried."

His eyes narrowed. "In a good or bad way?"

"Well, good, I think." I shrugged. "Freaked out at first, then treated me like I was made of glass. But in the meeting, he said he felt like the condom breaking was him coming inside me without my consent." I gave him a sad smile. "He said the idea of that makes him feel ill."

Cory gave my hand a squeeze, but then I noticed Amon's eyes flinch and he pressed his lips together.

"Something to add?" I asked him.

Cory shot Amon a look, then focused back at me. "What?"

I slumped back in my chair. "Nothing. Sorry. I'm just . . ." I sighed. I didn't know how the fuck I was. "Ignore me."

"It's different for us," Amon said quietly, his deep voice low. Cory and I both looked at him. He shrugged and kept his gaze straight ahead. "For the top, I mean. It's our responsibility to make sure we care for you. You say he treated you like you were made of glass? So he fucking should. He should be worried for you, and he should do everything he can to make sure you're okay. Because that's what a good top does. And the consent thing? Makes him a good guy, yes? What you do for us is a gift of trust, and if he wasn't worried, if he didn't treat you like you were made of glass, then you'd have a problem."

I stared at him, blown away by every single word he said.

Cory smiled and leaned into him, his small hand engulfed by Amon's large one, and Amon kissed the side of his head.

I patted Cory's arm. "You can keep him," I said.

Then Keats appeared in the hall. "Sorry to make you wait."

I stood up. "Feeling better about what she said?"

He nodded and even managed a proper smile. "Yeah. I'm sorry I freaked out before."

I walked over to him and offered him my hand, but he collected me in a hug instead, breathing in deep. "Are you okay?" he murmured. "What do you need?"

Amon's words were fresh in my mind.

I looked up at Keats and smiled. "Nothing."

He rubbed my back but looked toward Cory and Amon before his eyes met mine. "What did you want to do? Are you hungry? Wanna grab something, or do you want to just go home? Maybe hit up a bar and get shitfaced?"

I laughed. "I don't mind." I looked back at Cory. "What are you guys doing?"

Cory stood up, pulling Amon to his feet, and he melted into his side. He fit exactly under Amon's chin. "We're going back to my place to finish what we barely started before you called."

I laughed. "We should get some takeout and go back to your place," I said to Keats. "And maybe talking about what happened tonight is a good idea."

He nodded. "Yeah."

We went out into the street, busy now with Friday night crowds. Cory gave me a hug. "I'll call you tomorrow."

"Thank you for coming down."

He smiled. "You'd do the same for me."

"I would."

"Are you still going shopping at IKEA tomorrow?"

"Yes," I answered quickly, before Keats could begin anymore self-doubts. I looked up at him. "Yes?"

He nodded and tightened his arm around my shoulder, as if he really did need that small confirmation of my still wanting to see him tomorrow.

I gave Cory a smile. "Be good." Then I looked over at Amon. "Give this man everything he wants."

Amon gave me a smirk as Cory slotted in under his arm and they walked away, and with a deep breath, I saw a pizza and kebab shop across the road and led Keats toward it. "Let's get pizza. I'm starving."

The Uber back to his place was quiet, though he kept hold of my hand on the backseat between us.

We really did need to talk, about a lot of things, but I'd learned a few things about Keats tonight.

And despite the circumstances, that wasn't a bad thing.

Did it change my mind about him?

Nope.

If anything, it made me fall for him a little bit harder.

CHAPTER NINE
KEATS

TONIGHT HAD NOT GONE HOW I'D PLANNED IT, at all.

Things had started out strong then gone to absolute shit, but walking back into my apartment, I got the feeling maybe it wasn't a complete write-off.

We needed to talk.

We needed to have some serious conversations. Some very real, not-easy conversations.

But first, we needed to eat.

I took the pizza to the coffee table and went to the kitchen. I grabbed two glasses for the soda, then some serviettes. It seemed easier to be busy because I wasn't sure if I was ready for what came next.

Though he did say he still wanted to go shopping tomorrow . . .

Which felt like a beacon at this point.

He flipped open the pizza box and all but inhaled half of the first piece. "Oh, this is really good," he said, his mouth half full. Then he laughed and patted the seat next to him. "Come sit down."

I did, and I managed one slice of pizza by the time he'd put his second away, but then he took a long drink and I knew it was time for talking.

"So," he began. "Tonight was fun."

I snorted. "Yeah, not really."

He knocked his knee to mine. "I think I learned a few things about you."

Oh dear.

"Uh, good or bad? Mostly bad, I'm guessing. God, I'm so sorry. I freaked out earlier."

"Hey," he murmured. "It's okay, Keats. You're entitled to freak out. It was kinda scary."

"You seemed to handle it just fine. Grace under fire, and all that."

He smiled at me. "Grace under fire," he repeated. "I like that. But no, I tend not to panic." He shrugged. "I mean, in the end it doesn't change anything."

"I'm more of a panic-now, think-rationally-later kind of guy."

Linden smiled and leaned into me a little. "I noticed."

"Sorry about that."

"There's nothing to be sorry about. Like I said, I learned some things about you. And as your boyfriend, that was probably overdue."

I was hit with relief and nerves. Mostly relief. "You still want to be my boyfriend?"

"Yes, of course. Why wouldn't I?"

"I dunno," I said with a shrug. "Because of what happened. Because I freaked out."

"You didn't really freak out," he offered gently. "Your panic was out of concern for me, and what you said about consent was very sweet."

Oh.

I tried to smile for him. "I just . . . I'm still sorry it happened."

"I am too." He slid his hand over mine. "We weren't ready for that kind of heavy situation. We'd just jumped straight into calling each other boyfriend without having talked about anything. Because it was new and exciting, and everything was perfect and shiny. And I think it was a pretty big wake-up call, no?"

I nodded. "Yeah."

"So while I wished it hadn't happened, it did. And now we have to deal with that. But yes, I still want to call you boyfriend. If you want that as well."

I nodded quickly and pulled his hand into my lap. "I do."

His smile was short-lived. "But we need to talk about the heavy stuff."

I held onto his hand, not wanting to let him go. "Yeah."

"If my results come back positive in three months," he hedged, "what would you do?"

"Well, to be completely honest, I'd probably freak out first. I tend to go to water in the beginning. I think we both saw that tonight." I held his hand in both of mine and met his eyes. "But it wouldn't change how I feel about you. That's one thing I did realise tonight."

He threaded his fingers with mine. "And how do you feel about me?"

I barked out a laugh. "Well, I feel giddy when I think about you, and I get butterflies. I want to touch you and hold you and talk to you all the time. I daydream about you at work, and I think about being with you all the time. Basically, if I'm breathing oxygen, I'm thinking about you." I laughed, embarrassed. Horrified at admitting this stuff out loud. "I don't know if it's love, Linden. I keep telling myself it's too soon. I can't possibly be in love with you so fast. So maybe I haven't fallen, per se. But I'm mid-fall. I'm falling in love with you. I told my mum about you, if that's any gauge. I mean, good lord. She already wants to meet you because I told her how amazing you are."

He stared at me, a stunned smile on his face.

"Oh, okay."

Oh hell.

"Was that too much? I can reel it back in if you need. I just—"

He barked out a laugh and squeezed my hand. "No, it's perfect. No reeling of anything in, thank you very much." His smile became something else. Something lovely. "I feel exactly the same, Keats. Giddy and like I'm buzzing the whole time. And I don't know if I've fallen in love with you already, and I haven't told my mother yet, but I did tell Cory I was going to marry you on like day two, I think. So if we want to have a contest about falling too fast, I think I might be winning."

I laughed, stunned. "You're going to marry me?"

He nodded. "After our first impromptu date and you gave me that serviette into a flower, I called Cory and was like, 'Uhhhh holy shit, this guy . . . I think I'm gonna marry him.' I mean, I named our hypothetical cats already."

I chuckled, feeling a little lightheaded. "Yeah. Meatball and Spaghetti."

Linden smiled and let out a sigh. "And if your results come back positive, it wouldn't change how I feel about you either. And I know that's easy to say right now, but I mean it, Keats. It would change how we do some things, but for the most part, it would be just something we live with. Something we monitor and take care of."

I squeezed his hand and nodded. "Exactly."

"And as for condoms in the future," he went on, "we need to get tested again in a couple of months, so I say we continue to use them until we get those results in. Then if we're comfortable in not using them, we can discuss that then."

I nodded. "Sounds like a very sensible plan."

"Thanks. I'm entering my very-sensible-middle-life-gay era."

I managed a smile.

"And," he added, "we're going to talk about our sexual histories, because that wasn't something we'd talked about before tonight when it was like, holy shit, I have no clue."

"Fair enough. Though to completely warn you, mine will be short and kinda boring."

He snorted. "Uh, excuse me. I've seen your dick. There's nothing short and boring about it."

I chuckled. "And we should probably talk about boyfriend things, like relationship dos and don'ts. I think we were going to discuss expectations tonight, but then the whole broken condom thing happened."

He grinned. "Okay, first list of dos," he said, taking another slice of pizza and biting into it. This time he chewed and swallowed before speaking. "Feeding me makes me a happy boyfriend."

I laughed. "Noted."

"I'm not really a clubbing or bar kind of guy. That era is over for me," he said. "So, nights on the couch with pizza and Netflix also makes me a happy boyfriend."

"Perfect."

"I'm not opposed to being spoiled." He sniffed. "Not in a sugar-daddy way, but showered with affection and attention."

I snorted. "Affection and attention I can do."

"And the paper flowers you've been making are the absolute sweetest thing ever, so I won't be opposed to that happening forever."

"I'll have to up my origami levels, but no pressure. Totally manageable."

"And the prostate orgasms and thorough railings." He nodded. "Also not opposed to those."

I laughed. "Right. No pressure there at all."

"What about your list of dos?"

I tried to think . . . "That smile you're wearing right now," I said. "Just to see you smile. That's it."

"That's it?" He looked a little horrified. "While that is sweet, and yes, I'll be telling Cory you said that, shouldn't you have actual goals?"

"I want to make you happy," I replied. "That makes me happy."

"That's not fair."

"But making you happy with food, Netflix, and sex, ticks a lot of boxes for me as well. That's pretty much all I need. And maybe coffee."

His grin was something spectacular. "Okay, coffee. Got it."

I made a face. "And my shop is a priority for me. There will be times when I can drop everything for you, and I absolutely will. But there will be times when I can't. And that won't be a reflection of how I feel or how much you mean to me. It will just simply mean that I can't leave the store that minute."

He nodded. "That is perfectly reasonable. See? You do have relationship dos."

"And what about your don'ts?"

He made a thoughtful face and hummed. "Hmm. Racism and bigotry of any kind."

"Of course."

"Treating anyone as if they're beneath you," he added. "That's a hard limit for me."

"Good. I agree."

"And leaving your stuff all over the floor like an animal or a feral teenager." He made a face. "Or like you expect someone else to pick up after you."

"Okay, that's fair." I held up my hand like it was a scout's honour thing. "I shall dutifully try to not leave my shit all over the floor. Like a grown up."

"Are you making fun of me?"

"Absolutely not."

He poked me. "Okay, I'm adding *making fun of Linden* to the list of boyfriend don'ts."

I laughed. "Noted."

"What are your boyfriend don'ts?"

"Making fun of Linden."

"I think you're failing on the first try."

I snorted. "I'm just kidding." I lifted his hand to my lips and kissed his knuckles. "I don't really have a list of don'ts. Just don't be a terrible person. Don't take me for granted. Don't assume I can read minds, because I can't. And I'm sorely out of practice at the boyfriend thing, so if you're upset over something, tell me. If you need something, tell me. If you have a problem, tell me. Don't lie to me. Don't be hating on pineapple on pizza—it's a valid topping choice. And don't speak ill of Beyoncé. That's it. That's my list."

Linden laughed. "Pineapple is—"

"Shh. It's on the don't list."

His grin was beautiful, and he sat back on the couch, looked at me, and sighed. "I'm glad we're okay, Keats. The broken condom wasn't an ideal thing to happen, but for what it's worth, if I had to go through this with someone, I'm glad it was you."

I swallowed and ran my thumb over his hand. "I wish it didn't happen either. But I'm glad we're okay. I thought you were going to tell me you needed space or time or that you didn't want to see me anymore. I thought I'd hurt you, and that made me just about want to puke."

He slid his hand to my jaw and leaned in to kiss me. "You are the sweetest man."

I took a deep breath in and sighed. "It was more than the consent thing. I mean, that's a big thing for me, obviously. But I feel like it's my job to take care of you, to look after you, and I failed. It's a responsibility thing. For me, at least." This was awkward to say out loud, but I needed to say this. "When you take me inside you, it's more than . . . I don't even know what I'm trying to say. You trust me to take care of you, and the responsibility is mine to make sure you're okay, and then when this happened, I know you said it's not my fault—and I do know that—but still, the responsibility . . . And I keep thinking, did I put it on too fast, did I compromise it with a hangnail, did I—"

"Hey," he whispered. "I get it. I do. Amon said something similar at the clinic. I get the responsibility thing, and I appreciate that. Just know that I don't blame you. You did nothing wrong."

I sighed, thankful for his words but still not sure I felt absolved just yet.

"Are you sure you still want to go shopping tomorrow? We can leave it. There's no rush." I looked around my lame apartment. "It's been like this for years. Another week or two won't hurt."

"Shopping tomorrow sounds fun. And honestly, the distraction will do us good. Our test results won't start to come in until next week, and we can't change what the results will be, so you know what? I think a day of shopping and lunch is just what we need."

God, he made me so happy. "Okay."

Linden looked at the pizza. "Have you had enough? You only had one piece." He handed me another slice, then closed the lid and picked up the remote. "Shall we watch something?"

I had to speak around my mouthful of pizza. "Whatever you wanna watch."

He laughed, settled in under my arm with his head on my chest, and began to scroll my recently watched list.

"Okay, we need to add 'Linden makes all TV selections' to our relationship list of dos."

I snorted. "That's fine. I never watch much anyway. I go to bed early because I'm up at half four."

He grimaced. "We're also adding *Keats does not wake Linden up when he leaves for work* to the list of don'ts." Then he amended, "Unless it's for sex. Then that's okay."

"One hundred percent adding that to my list."

"Waking me up?"

"For sex, yes. Not because I'm being loud at four thirty in the morning."

"You can be loud during sex."

I sighed. "This list is getting longer and longer."

He laughed, then pointed the remote at the TV. "Ooh, I haven't seen this. It's about gay pirates. Should we watch?"

"Gay pirates? Absolutely, one hundred percent."

LINDEN SPENT THE NIGHT AT MY PLACE. IT WAS always the plan, though I thought that might change after the condom incident.

But nope. He wanted to stay. He wanted to sleep in my

bed, wake up for a casual breakfast, and then spend the morning at IKEA.

It seemed while nothing between us had changed, everything had.

Being somewhat pessimistic by nature, I was inclined to assume things would change for the worse.

But maybe things had changed for the better?

I was afraid to admit this out loud, of course. But we'd talked. We'd discussed what-if scenarios and we'd talked about our expectations moving forward.

Like grown-ups. Like people who were serious about making this work.

Was the condom breaking ideal?

Absolutely not.

In fact, I wished it hadn't happened at all.

But out of a bad situation came something good. A silver lining to a rather dark cloud.

I dared to think we'd be okay. Better, even.

Was it still too early for declarations of love and forever?

Realistically, yes.

But something inside me knew this was real.

"You okay?" Linden waved his hand in front of my face. "Ready to go shopping? Or still need more coffee?"

I laughed and nodded out the windscreen to the entrance of IKEA. "I'm ready. Not sure my bank account is, but I am."

He laughed. "You don't have to buy anything. We can just look. It'll be fun."

We got out of my work van and he held his hand out for me to hold. Was I the hand-holding-in-public kind of guy? Not before him, no. But now? Hell yes, I wanted to hold his hand.

He grinned as I threaded our fingers and he did a little

happy-bouncy walk as we went through the doors. He was such a ball of energy and fun, and I swear it was contagious.

He made me happy.

"Sooo," he said as we reached the first room. "New couch, or other furniture?"

I grimaced. "Uh . . . Do I need a new couch?" I probably did. My couch was old . . .

He snorted. "No, no. Your couch is fine. Do you like this?"

I looked around. "I mean, I like it all. It all looks great, but . . ."

He smiled at me with all the patience of a saint. "Okay, so how about we just look at everything with no intention to buy. No pressure."

"Am I that bad at this?"

He laughed. "Heavens no. How about this: I narrow it down to three setting options—coffee table, bookcase, cabinet or whatever—and you choose out of one of those?"

I sighed, relieved. "Perfect."

He really was good at this.

He opted for three different rooms, each with furniture with lighter coloured frames, nothing big and bulky because I needed to work with a smaller space and minimal light.

I liked all three but preferred one over the others. "I like this one," I said. "But maybe I should get the sofa as well. And maybe some frames for the walls. And the rug. God, this is why they do it like this, isn't it? So you can see it all together and just buy it all."

Linden laughed. "Pretty much, yeah."

We took all the product numbers and item codes we needed, and I stood in the aisle. "Hm, maybe we could take a look in the kitchen area. It's always fun."

His grin widened, and taking my hand, he pulled me

along. We looked at different settings and utensils. He laughed when I picked up the dinosaur ladle and the penguin egg holder. He might have thought I was joking, but nope. "I'm totally getting these."

And then we found the pet section. "Oh my god," he said, finding the biggest cat fort on the planet. "Meatball and Spaghetti are totally having this. They can have their own room with their beds and toys."

"Our hypothetical cats get their own room?"

He nodded very seriously. "Oh, yes. With a big window for sunlight and heated beds in winter."

"So you'll be the dad that spoils them then."

"Yep. And you'll be the dad that cleans the litter boxes."

"Thanks."

He laughed. "You're welcome."

"And this hypothetical place we're getting . . ." I said, trying to ignore the thump of my heart. "With a room for our hypothetical cats, is there a hypothetical budget for this? A hypothetical room for the furniture I'm about to buy, perhaps? Because I don't particularly want to pay for all this twice."

Linden leaned up on his toes and gave me a quick, smiley kiss. "I'll make it work."

I wanted to ask him if he had a hypothetical timeframe in mind but was too afraid. What if he said he was just joking? What if he said next month?

I didn't know which answer scared me the most.

After the pet section, he found the plant section. He went straight past the artificial plants to a table of small real succulents. He picked up a euphorbia. "Oh, my god. Look at how cute he is. He's coming home with me." Then he picked up a second one. "You need one too."

"Well," I hedged. "That's a euphorbia. They won't be good for Meatball and Spaghetti."

Linden gasped and put the plants back. His gaze shot to mine. "Then which ones can we have?"

For our cats that didn't exist?

"Uh, this one." I picked up a haworthia. "These are fine."

"Then we'll have two of these." He selected two. "I'm so glad you know which ones to get. I could have made them sick."

The whole hypothetical cats thing had started out funny, but it was starting to sound serious. "So about these cats," I hedged, not entirely sure of what I even wanted to ask.

"Rescues, of course. From the RSPCA or a shelter. They don't have to be kittens. Everyone loves kittens, so maybe we should look at some of the older ones that get overlooked."

"You're serious about them?"

He stopped, and his eyes met mine. "I am. Aren't you?"

"Serious about the cats? Or about us?"

His blue eyes searched mine, his hands fell to his sides. "Both? Either? None?"

Oh jeez. "Both," I whispered. "Definitely both."

He grinned, then gave me a gentle shove. "You scared me."

I laughed. "Sorry. I wasn't sure if you were joking or if you were serious. I mean, the cats having their own room implied us living together, and I didn't know what to make of that. I'm the overthinking type, Linden. So when you say stuff like that, I have seven tabs open in my brain working at the same time, running possible outcomes and scenarios."

His smile was slow to spread. "Just seven tabs?"

"Two are someone working an FBI whiteboard of scenarios, one's a Venn diagram, two are spreadsheets, one's running a video reel of *Love Actually*, and the last one is breathing into a paper bag."

Linden laughed, then leaned up to give me another quick kiss. "You're so fucking perfect."

Before I could argue with that, his phone rang. He put the two succulents into my basket, and I saw Cory's name on the screen before he answered the call.

"Hello, gorgeous. . . . Yes, we're both great today. . . . No, no results yet. . . . Oh? Is that right?" He grinned at me. "Well, he was very sweet. . . . Of course I approve. . . . No, we're in IKEA. . . . Okay, talk to you then. Bye."

He pocketed his phone and sighed. "Well, our little trip to the clinic last night prompted Cory and Amon to discuss a few things. I'll get all the details later, but I think it was the exclusivity talk."

"Oh. Good for them. Amon seemed nice. Sorry I was not my most amicable when I met him."

He waved me off. "Don't apologise. He was lovely, and I told Cory I approve. What he said last night helped me understand you a little better, I think."

I stopped. "Really?"

"Yep. Just about how a top should treat his boyfriend. I said you were worried about me, and Amon said so you should be. But then you basically said the same thing last night too. It's about responsibility and care, and it just proved what decent guys you and Amon are."

"Oh. Right." I tried not to be embarrassed. "Did you not think I was decent before?"

"Of course I did. But it was just good to hear it, ya know?" He let out a deep breath and smiled up at me. "I like that you looked after me, that I was your first concern."

Maybe the middle of IKEA was not the best place for this conversation, because I wanted to pull him in close, wrap my arms around him, and kiss him. Instead, I just stared into his eyes and hoped he could see the sincerity in mine. "You are."

He smiled serenely as if he needed to hear me say that. "Have you had enough shopping for one day?"

"Yep. But this has been fun."

"It has!"

"Just so we're clear," I added, "the fun part of this shopping trip also includes when it gets delivered and you helping me put it all together, right?"

"Absolutely. I'm more than happy to supervise and help by telling you if you're doing something wrong."

I snorted. "Awesome."

He did a little happy wiggle, then looked around. "Okay, how do we get out of here?"

We found the counter, I bought what was in the basket, ordered the rest to be delivered, and Linden bought us lunch on the way home.

We spent the afternoon at his place, kissing in the kitchen, cuddling on the couch, and laughing along with the gay pirate show. It was utter perfection. We still hadn't had anymore test results come in yet, but that wasn't surprising.

Not that it would change how I felt about him.

My heart was already in this.

I was falling for him, if I hadn't fallen completely already.

When it was time for me to go, he walked me to the door and sighed with a frown. "I wish you could stay," he murmured.

"Maybe next time," I said. I had an early start in the morning and hadn't brought any clothes with me. I put my fingers to his chin and lifted his face so I could kiss him. "I wish I had a paper flower to give you," I said. "For this weekend, for what you mean to me."

"What flower would it be?"

I thought for a second. "A peach blossom."

"What does it mean?"

I searched his eyes, my heart in my throat. *"My heart is thine."*

He closed his eyes slowly and breathed in deep before looking up at me with big doe eyes. "My heart is thine. My heart is also thine . . . thou . . . thoust?" He shrugged. "Yours."

I chuckled and kissed him again, pressing my lips to his, soft and slow. God, I wished I could stay. I never wanted to leave him. I groaned at the door. "You know, if we had that hypothetical place for our hypothetical cats already, I wouldn't have to leave."

"If we had our own place," he murmured, "you and I would be in bed all afternoon. And we wouldn't need to be worrying about condoms."

I groaned louder and took a step back. "Well, that's not helping."

He laughed. "Sorry."

"You're absolutely not."

"Absolutely not at all."

I opened his door, making myself leave, because if I didn't leave right now, I wasn't leaving at all. "On that note," I said. "I'd like it known that this is a discernible effort on my part in making myself leave. A strength of will, if you like."

He laughed. "I'll call you later tonight," he murmured, peeking shyly around his door. "And just so you know, there will be phone sex. The fact that I'm not dragging you to my room right now is testament to the strength of *my* will, if you like."

I grinned at him. "Okay then."

"Bye, Keats."

I nodded and he closed his door, and I stood there for a few seconds trying to catch my breath. I put my hand to my chest and smiled at his door, and I heard him laugh, so I was pretty sure he was watching me through his peephole.

"Have a good night," I said to his door.

"If I open this door, you're not leaving," came his reply.

I laughed. "Okay, okay. I'm going." I took a step back down the hall, assuming he was still watching me through his peephole. I waved. "Night."

Then I had to make myself leave. And I had to make myself stop smiling. But I set my little plant up on the shelf next to Elizabeth and gave him a welcome drink. Then I took out my new dinosaur ladle and penguin egg cooker, happy that I'd bought them. Doing something fun was long overdue.

Then I looked around my lounge room, at the tired couch, the old table, the even older TV stand.

My new furniture would be arriving next weekend. For my new outlook on life.

For the new me.

The me who knew it was about time to start living.

Part of me felt that I had already started. This new phase of my life was looking bright. And I could tell myself that Linden wasn't the sole reason or the centre of my happiness; that it had to come from within.

But oh boy, he was a big part of it. And in the unlikely chance that he wasn't in my life forever, I'd be okay. This new me, the me that wasn't solely focused on work, the guy who now looked up every once in a while, would be okay.

I GOT TO WORK THE NEXT MORNING WITH A VAN full from the flower market. Like every morning, Robbie handed me a coffee and Lina began unloading the van.

"How was your weekend?" Robbie asked, looking me up and down. "You look suspiciously happy."

I laughed. Jeez, how to explain my weekend? "Well, it started out kinda bad but it ended pretty well."

"Bad? What happened?"

I winced, unsure if I should tell him . . . then realised if anyone would understand, it would be him. We both collected one box each and I glanced around to see Lina already back inside. "Broken condom," I whispered.

Robbie grimaced. "Oh. Did you go get—"

"Yep. Rapid tests were all negative. Expecting more results yet, obviously."

"And you and he are okay?"

"Yeah, we talked about everything." I slid the box onto the shelf in the cool room. "Actually, I think we're better than okay. Not an ideal start to a relationship, but at least we know we can handle the big stuff. Know what I mean?"

He slid his box on the shelf and gave me a clap on the shoulder. "Sounds serious."

"It is. We've established the boyfriend title."

"Wow."

Lina appeared with another box. "No, honestly, it's fine. You two stay in here and chat. I'll do all the work."

I snorted. "Sorry."

Robbie clicked his tongue. "Go easy on him. He's in love."

Lina huffed but relented a smile. "Is he still wonderful?"

I nodded, feeling foolishly giddy. "He is."

"I'm happy for you." Then she raised both eyebrows. "But the van won't unload itself."

I laughed, but Robbie and I unloaded the rest of the van without complaint. We had our order lists to get through and everyone settled into work, humming along to the radio, getting as much done as we could before the doors opened, before the phone began to ring off the hook.

"Lina," I called out. "I need ideas."

"What for?"

"Flowers for Linden."

"Paper flowers?"

"Yeah, possibly. Maybe something else that says something more. I don't know."

"More . . ." she mused. "Like a declaration of a hundred red roses but not a hundred red roses."

"Exactly."

"Get some red paper and make him a red rose."

I shrugged. "I could . . . and he really does love the paper flowers I've given him. He keeps them on the shelf in his living room. But I think it's lost the charm."

"You can get flower LEGOs now," Robbie piped up with.

Hmm.

"Or a dozen cupcakes with frosting to look like flowers," Lina suggested.

I sighed. "I don't know. I want to give him something with significance. Not necessarily grand or expensive. Something small and meaningful."

"A picture in a frame," Lina said. "Of a flower that tells him how you feel. Make it a series of different flowers, but hand drawn and in matching frames."

I thought about it, then considered it some more. "I like that idea. That could totally work." Then I thought about it a little longer and gave Lina my best sad puppy dog eyes. "Where do I begin to look for that?"

Lina sighed. "You let me look for it, that's what you do."

I grabbed her hand. "I will be eternally thankful."

She raised an unimpressed eyebrow. "I dunno about eternally grateful, but what you can be is fulfilling my orders this morning."

"Deal. Maybe a list of three or four collections and I'll veto, of course."

Now she stared. "Why do I feel like I was coerced into this?"

"Because you were," Robbie said flatly. He put a bunch of daffodils into a holder. "And you, Keats. Wanting something with a significant meaning but making someone else buy it. For shame."

I gestured to myself. "Would you trust me to pick out anything? We went to IKEA and I bought a dinosaur ladle and a penguin egg cooker."

Robbie blinked, then pursed his lips at Lina. "Google watercolour prints at the Blue Door Gallery in Paddington. They have an array of painted antique cards." Then he side-eyed me as he slotted another bunch of daffodils into the holder. "You're welcome."

I took Lina's clipboard and began her orders. I found myself looking for a chance to catch Robbie alone. "Can I ask you something?"

"Of course."

"You and Tan. You've been together for years, right?" He nodded. "When did you know? That he was . . . that you were in it for the long haul?"

He put the last of the tulips in their holders, turned to me, and smiled. "Day one. Before I even met him. It was a party, and I saw him come into the bar with his friends. Now, he will tell you a different story. He will tell you I played hard to get and that I wasn't interested, but I can tell you right now, I knew he was the one for me before I'd even met him."

I couldn't believe it.

"You never told me that."

"Because it was foolish and we never got together that night. I mean, we got together," he said, his eyes wide. "If you know what I mean. But the next morning we went our separate ways, as we've all done. And we ran into each other a few days later, and the weekend after that. Some might call that fate. Well, Tan would call it fate. Others, being me, might call that asking around, finding out where he hung out and where he worked, and putting myself in his path."

"So you stalked him?"

"No. I just heard in certain circles about places he may or may not have frequented, and I found myself locationally curious."

I laughed. "Right."

He rolled his eyes. "Then we played the coy game, not interested but really so very interested, and he told me if I was serious, I had to take him out on a proper date. And the rest is history. We've been together almost six years. That's forever in gay years. Like dog years but for gays."

I sighed happily. "I . . . I really do like Linden. I really do think it could be serious."

"And the condom breakage?" he whispered.

I groaned. "Yeah, not ideal. But it was also a bit of a wake-up call. We were so busy being all new and shiny that we'd skipped the serious, non-shiny stuff, ya know?"

He nodded. "It's easy to do."

"It made us talk it all out, and we're good. We're going to deal with it together."

"Keats," Lina called out from the service counter. "They have all kinds. Which kinds of flower paintings are you after?"

"Peach blossom, green carnations, white jonquil, white pansy, and a kumquat tree."

Robbie laughed, but he shook his head. "That's oddly specific."

"Yeah, I don't like your chances," Lina mumbled. "Oh, wait. They can do commissions or requests."

"Do it."

"It's going to be fairly exxy."

"It's fine." He's totally worth it. But that also probably meant I wouldn't be getting them this week. "If there's a wait, I might have to make him some more paper flowers in the interim."

Robbie sighed. "My god, you really do have it bad."

I shot him a glare. "How are your origami skills?"

CHAPTER TEN
LINDEN

KEATS WAS SO STINKING CUTE. HE WAS SO undeniably adorable and thoughtful, and every day that passed was a day I fell harder into love.

Because over the course of the week, our test results came in.

On Tuesday, the syphilis and gonorrhoea results arrived in our inbox, and he sent me two neatly folded almond blossom paper flowers. Negative, for us both.

The note with it read, Almond blossom for a promise.

On Wednesday, the hepatitis results came in and he sent me a tiny origami white flower.

White heather for strength the note read.

Then on Friday, the chlamydia results arrived, and he sent me a yellow origami blossom. *Celandine for the joys to come in our future*, the handwritten note read.

All our tests so far were negative and while I was not surprised, I was still relieved.

He'd come to my place on Wednesday and he'd grinned, pleased with himself when I showed him the small botanical display of paper flowers.

"You like them?" he'd asked.

"I love them," I'd replied. "I'll need to find a better way to display them, maybe get a glass case. But they're my absolute favourite thing in the world."

He'd wrapped me up in a slow hug and breathed me in, simply content to hold me. He never hinted at more, never pushed for sex, not since the condom incident. It wasn't any kind of big deal, and I was more than happy to spend the night curled up on the couch with him, eating takeout and watching funny TV shows.

But on Friday when he knocked on my door, I'd barely got *hello* out before he stepped inside and collected me for a hug. The kind of hug that slotted us together, two halves of the one whole. Slow and unhurried, no urgency, no desperation, just a 'god, I missed you' hug.

"You okay?" I mumbled into his neck.

"Hm," he replied, pulling back and lifting my chin so he could crush his mouth to mine in a filthy kiss. He pulled my body to his, flush and hard in all the right places, then he pushed me up against the wall near the door.

"Was a week too long?" I asked, when we broke for air.

He stopped kissing my neck. "I'm trying to take it slow."

I ran my hands down over his arse and ground our hips together. "And how's that working out for you?"

His breath was half groan, half chuckle. "Poorly. And I was doing so well until you opened the door."

I pushed him back a fraction and pinched his chin. "After all the paper flower gifts you sent me this week, you're gonna be having a lot of sex this weekend, so if you wanted to start now, I would not be opposed."

He let out a breathy groan. "Linden," he murmured, a tortured sound.

I met his gaze. "Are you worried about what happened

before?" I asked. "I bought new condoms, if you're concerned..."

He shook his head. "No. I just want to know you're sure. One hundred percent."

I ran my hands down his back to his arse and pulled him flush against me. "One hundred percent."

He kissed me, hard, and inhaled deeply, his eyes closed. "Thank god. I'm so ready." Then he grabbed my hand and led me to my bedroom. He pushed me back onto my bed, then proceeded to undress me, one torturous piece of clothing at a time.

When I was completely naked before him, he knelt between my thighs. He'd somehow lost his shoes and his shirt, but his jeans were still on.

Christ, he was hot.

"I don't know how I could go months at a time without sex," he murmured. "Before you. I never missed it. I never craved it. Now, with you, it's been one week and I'm losing my mind." He leaned over me, brushing his nose to mine. "I can't get enough of you."

"You can have me as often as you need," I said, popping the button on his jeans. "But you're still incredibly overdressed."

He kissed me, bruising lips and hot tongue. I was lifting my hips, rocking, trying to find friction.

More, more, more.

"Keats," I hissed.

He got the hint. He scrambled out of his jeans and dropped the lube and condoms on the bed. He worked me over, prepping me and getting me ready, until I was slick and panting with need.

Then he spread my thighs, lifted my arse, positioned his cock, and pushed into me. He kept one hand on my forehead, his eyes locked with mine, watching for every flicker of emotion, every feeling, every cue I could give him.

He took me slow and steady. With more patience than I had, with me his only concern.

When I'd adjusted to the size of him, to the most intimate breach, he began to move. Slow and deep, in and out, so much tenderness and care.

When he began to move faster—the pain of his restraint in his eyes, on his furrowed brow—I kissed him. "Faster, harder, Keats. I need more."

It wasn't for me. It was for him.

He squinted his eyes shut and groaned. "Fuck. I'm trying to . . . take my time."

I rolled my hips, meeting his thrust. God, I could feel every inch of him. "Take me however you want me," I whispered.

His fingers dug into my arse; he bucked into me and held it. I could feel his cock throb, and when he cried out, I could feel him spill into the condom.

Oh, hell yes.

I pulled his face to mine, thrusting my tongue into his mouth, and he shuddered as he rode out the waves of his orgasm.

So fucking hot.

He collapsed on top of me, his breathing ragged, and he let out a breathy laugh. "I was imagining that going a lot better," he mumbled. "A lot longer, anyway. You didn't come. I'm sorry."

"It's okay," I said with a chuckle. "You can suck my dick later."

He laughed and pulled back to look at me, his eyes now a glazed-over kind of serene. "Deal."

He pulled out of me, careful that the condom had remained intact. Of course it had. And he disposed of it.

"Hey," I hedged as he came back to bed. "Just a question. You don't need to answer right now, but have a think and we can discuss it."

He slid in beside me and wrapped me up in his arms, kissing my lips, my forehead. Clearly still enjoying his afterglow. "Ask away."

"You were worried about the condom." It wasn't really a question . . .

"Sure. I've never had one break before, so I never really worried about it until now."

"But we've been tested," I added.

He pulled back so he could meet my gaze. "Yes. But we still don't have the official HIV results yet."

"I know. And that's perfectly fine. If it comes back for one of us as positive, then there'll be medications and more tests, and maybe we'll be using condoms forever, and that's completely fine. But if we both come back as negative . . ."

"You don't want to use condoms?"

"I don't want you to have to worry about one breaking," I explained. "Trying to go slow, trying to be careful. I want you to enjoy what we do and not be cautious or inhibit yourself because you're worried about me." I shrugged. "I can take PrEP. If that becomes an option for us. If that's something we're both comfortable with. Maybe not now, but in a few months' time, or a year from now, or five years from now."

He began to smile. "Five years from now?"

Oh jeez.

"Well, yes. Considering we'll be living together by then with our two cats and our array of plants."

He chuckled. "I'm glad you're thinking ahead like me. About living together, one day. About how my plans now include you. Us."

"And Meatball and Spaghetti."

He snorted. "Of course."

"One day. Soon?"

His eyes met mine and he kissed me softly. "One day. Soon." The corner of his lips lifted in a half smile. "Soooooooon."

I chuckled, feeling all kinds of happy. And unsated. "Now, about that dick sucking?"

He laughed and manoeuvred himself between my legs. He pulled the bedcovers up over himself so I couldn't see what he was doing. Then his warm, wet mouth surrounded me. As much as I wanted to see, being deprived and simply feeling what he did to me was so, so good.

"Fuck yes," I hissed as he began to pump the shaft and suck on the head.

Then his fingers were in my arse and he tapped that magic button inside me. I came so hard and so fast, I almost blacked out.

Every fibre of my being was on fire and somehow liquid at the same time. I convulsed and shuddered for the better part of half a minute afterward. Long after he'd wrapped me up in his arms and soothed me.

Christ almighty.

He let me doze on his chest, rubbing soft circles on my back, his fingers in my hair.

"I love you," he murmured.

I wondered if I'd imagined him saying it, if I'd dreamed it. The way my heart rate took off, I was certain he'd said it out loud.

He kissed the side of my head. "I know it's probably too soon for me to drop such a huge declaration," he added gently. "But it's true. I've never felt this way about anyone, Linden. I can't imagine anyone more perfect for me than you."

I looked up at him, needing to see his face, his eyes. "I love you too. I don't expect things to be this good all the time, and I don't know what our future will hold, but god, I'm ready to find out."

His smile was breathtaking. He stroked the side of my face with his fingertip. "I'm ready to find out too."

"Well, I think getting your furniture delivery tomorrow and us putting all those flat packs together will be the real test. If we can get through that, we can get through anything."

He laughed. "True. But I think we'll be fine. I'm pretty sure I'll do anything you ask me, anything you say."

I was grinning at him. "Are you entering your whipped boyfriend era?"

He put his head back down, tightened his hold on me. "One hundred percent."

EPILOGUE
LINDEN

THREE MONTHS LATER

"PLEASE BE CAREFUL WITH THOSE," I SAID TO THE removalist guys. It was an open box with six beautiful frames and the glass display case of my origami flowers. "They're very special. Break anything else and I won't care."

Keats laughed as he slid another box onto the kitchen counter. "They're not *that* special."

I gasped and moved the box protectively closer to my chest. "Don't talk about them like that."

The biggest of the removalist pair gave me an odd look as he walked out. They were almost done, and then we could get organising. We could get settled in.

It was agreed without saying that Keats would do most of the lifting and the organising would be on me. After all, organising was what I did. The first thing the removalists had brought in was our bed, and I'd had it made before they'd brought in the second lot of boxes.

Yes, we were moving in together. Almost four months to the day since our first date.

Four months of perfection.

And we kept questioning the speed of it, but there was no denying how right it felt. Even our closest friends and our families admitted we were such a great fit. Like we'd been together for four years, not four months.

My mum had had her reservations in the beginning. When I'd told her how serious Keats and I were, she was wary. Then she met him. She saw how much he loved me, the way he treated me. She saw what a wonderful guy he was, and more importantly, she saw how we were together.

Then when I'd mentioned that we were considering moving in together when Keats' lease was up, she was over the moon for us.

Same with Keats' mum. She adored me, and she loved how happy I made her son.

And our friends were happy for us too. Also happy that we'd found a two-bedroom apartment in Broadway, close to cafés, restaurants, the city.

"Where do you want this?" Amon asked, holding a rather large box full of my work folders.

"In the first bedroom," I replied. "Thank you!"

Cory was behind him, holding a smaller box for the kitchen. "Those removalists are hot," he whispered, fanning his face.

I rolled my eyes. "Like you don't have your own huge man taking care of you."

He grinned. "Oh, I know. I can still appreciate the view."

The removalists came in with Keats' new couch, and Keats came in after with another box. "These are your work folders, babe," he said. "Spare room?"

"Yes, please."

Amon appeared and Cory quickly slotted himself into his side. He looked almost childlike under Amon's huge arm, given their size difference. But man, Cory had never been this happy. I couldn't help but smile at the two of them together.

Then the removalist guy wheeled in a trolley with all our plants. "Veranda?"

"Yes, please."

The other removalist guy came in, said that was everything off the truck, and they left us in a new apartment with boxes and furniture everywhere. I'd never been this excited at the prospect of so much work.

"First things first," I said. "Before we order food and stop working." I held up the first frame. It was a simple white frame with an expertly displayed picture. It was actually an antique heavy paper card with a hand-painted watercolour green carnation.

It matched perfectly the other four. Keats had gifted me these when our final HIV tests came back. They were negative, but he'd arranged these prints prior, regardless of the result, to prove his love wouldn't change.

Five hand-painted flowers.

Green carnation, Austrian rose, peach blossom, a kumquat tree, and a single red rose.

Gay. Thou art all that is lovely. This heart is thine. Luck and prosperity, and a laugh at the kum-quick-tree memory.

And *eternal love*.

That was the night I'd asked him to move in with me. We'd talked about it, we'd joked about it. But I wanted to make it happen. I wanted to spend my life with him, so living together was a good place to start.

His lease would be up in two months, so he'd opted not to renew it. I'd given notice on my unit, and together we'd found this gorgeous two-bedroom apartment.

I hung the five frames along the entry wall so they'd be in full view of the kitchen and living room.

Keats came out, stretching his back and dusting his hands off. "All your work stuff is in the spare room," he said. He wiped his forehead with the back of his hand as he noticed the frames up already. He grinned at me. "Perfect."

"They really are."

"Yes," Cory said flatly. "You set the bar ridiculously high for the rest of us, Keats. You need to stop it."

Amon chuckled, giving Cory a bit of a jostle. "Do you not get spoiled enough?"

Cory looked up at him, his cheeks pink. "Never enough."

Amon gave him a look, and I was sure if we weren't there, he'd have kissed him. Amon was the quiet, private type, even though Cory told me he was very different when they were alone. I saw glimpses of that side of him every now and then, and he was relaxing around us more and more.

I really did like Amon, he was perfect for Cory, and I had to wonder how long it would be until they were moving in together.

Soon, hopefully.

"You know what?" Keats said. "I say we leave the other boxes for now. Let's order some pizza and sit down. We can tackle the rest tomorrow." He smiled at me. "We have forever."

My heart did that silly little skip it did when he said stuff like that. "We do."

He slid some boxes from the dining table to the floor and stretched his back. "I'm not cut out for removalist work. My poor body."

"I'll give you a massage later," I said.

Keats ordered some pizza from a wood-fire place down the block, and the four of us sat in our new place, surrounded by boxes and smiles . . . until the intercom buzzed.

New apartment, new intercoms, new everything, it was exciting, if not exhausting. I pressed the button. "Hello?"

"Delivery for McCulloch and Acres."

Keats McCulloch and Linden Acres.

I grinned at him, hearing our names together like that . . . "Are we expecting anything?"

"Oh, shit," he said, shoving the pizza crust in his mouth and standing up. "Let them up."

I buzzed them through. "Did you order something?"

"Ah, yeah. Maybe. When we got the move-in date. And then I forgot about it."

He went to the door, and a second later, a man wearing blue overalls pushed a rather large sized box in on a trundle trolley. I saw the word IKEA first, then the diagram on the side of the box.

It was the cat climbing house.

"Keats," I whispered.

He'd signed for the delivery and saw the delivery guy out while I stood there looking at it. "For real?"

Keats gave me a crushing hug. "For real."

Cory patted my arm. "We're gonna go," he said. "It's your first night here. You should spend it together."

I nodded, giving him a hug. "Thank you for helping today."

"You'll have to return the favour when it's my turn," he mumbled as we hugged.

"Soon."

He pulled back, then gave Keats a hug, and before Amon could be embarrassed, Cory dragged him out the door.

Then it was just me and Keats. "You bought this," I began.

"Because you wanted it." He pulled me in for a kiss. "I will always try to get you everything you want."

My eyes burned but I refused to cry. I was too happy to cry.

Keats held my face. "I thought we could get everything

unpacked and settled in. Enjoy having the place to ourselves for a bit, then maybe start looking at cat rescues."

I nodded, those stubborn tears finally winning the fight. "Okay." I wiped at my face. "I love you, Keats."

He thumbed a tear from my cheek. "I love you."

I gave myself a moment to really bask in his love. "Did you hear how the delivery guy said our names? McCulloch and Acres. I like how it sounded."

"I just put both our names on the delivery in case one of us was out or something."

"I think we should put both our names on everything."

"The electricity bill isn't so romantic."

I chuckled, and when I met his eyes, all I could do was sigh. "We need to test the shower for hot water and water pressure," I said. "Then we can see about that massage."

Meatball and Spaghetti arrived two weeks later.

We found them at the RSPCA. Two brothers, both tortoise shell, and approximately a year old. We needn't have worried about which name went to which cat.

One was a weirdo. He did burnouts, sliding skids around corners, and parkour on the furniture, all in the first twenty minutes of being home. He was definitely a Meatball.

Spaghetti was quieter, more refined, and looked at Meatball with a resignation that only siblings could manage.

They took to their new home, and to us, as if they'd been here with us forever. They loved their climbing gym. Well, Meatball loved it more. Spaghetti preferred chasing the best nap positions in the autumn sun across the floor in the living room from sunup to sundown.

They both loved cuddles with us on the couch in front of the TV with blankets. And they settled in from the very beginning, much like me and Keats.

Like this was how it was always supposed to be.

How it was always going to be.

I had no doubt this was a forever thing.

"Whatcha thinking about?" Keats asked me quietly. We were on the couch, the cats curled up on us, like we did every night. Keats had his head on my shoulder.

"Thinking about you," I replied. "About us."

"Oh?"

"Yeah. Thinking how perfect it is with these two." I gave Spaghetti a scratch under his ear. "Thinking about how perfect it is with you." I kissed the top of his head. "Thinking about forever."

Keats sat up, his eyes meeting mine. "Forever, huh?"

I grinned at him. "This is my cat-dad, domestic-bliss era. Pretty sure it's a forever kind of thing."

Keats leaned over and kissed me. "One hundred percent."

~FIN

FLORIOGRAPHY

The meanings of flowers have changed over time, and most flowers have different meanings for different cultures, and eras. Many flowers have multiple meanings.

Some of the Victorian Floriography used in this book:

- White clover – think of me
- Mulberry – I will not survive you
- Peach blossom – this heart is thine
- White poplar – time
- Sweet pea – delicate pleasures
- Hibiscus – delicate beauty
- Mezereon – desire to please
- Jonquil – please return my affection
- Wild pansy – think of me

Newer meanings

- White hyacinth – loveliness
- White clover – think of me
- Amaryllis – incredibly beautiful
- Lavender rose - enchantment

Sweet pea
Gorse
Tansy
Spurge
Blue vetch
Mint
Meadow bindweed
Knapweed
Clover
Chamomile
Hemlock
Salvia

If you liked Bloom...

If you enjoyed this book, you'll love
Throwing Hearts!

About the Author

N.R. Walker is an Australian author, who loves her genre of gay romance. She loves writing and spends far too much time doing it, but wouldn't have it any other way.

She is many things: a mother, a wife, a sister, a writer. She has pretty, pretty boys who live in her head, who don't let her sleep at night unless she gives them life with words.

She likes it when they do dirty, dirty things... but likes it even more when they fall in love. She used to think having people in her head talking to her was weird, until one day she happened across other writers who told her it was normal.

She's been writing ever since...

nrwalker.net

ALSO BY N.R. WALKER

Blind Faith

Through These Eyes (Blind Faith #2)

Blindside: Mark's Story (Blind Faith #3)

Ten in the Bin

Gay Sex Club Stories 1

Gay Sex Club Stories 2

Point of No Return – Turning Point #1

Breaking Point – Turning Point #2

Starting Point – Turning Point #3

Element of Retrofit – Thomas Elkin Series #1

Clarity of Lines – Thomas Elkin Series #2

Sense of Place – Thomas Elkin Series #3

Taxes and TARDIS

Three's Company

Red Dirt Heart

Red Dirt Heart 2

Red Dirt Heart 3

Red Dirt Heart 4

Red Dirt Christmas

Cronin's Key

Cronin's Key II

Cronin's Key III

Cronin's Key IV - Kennard's Story

Exchange of Hearts

The Spencer Cohen Series, Book One

The Spencer Cohen Series, Book Two

The Spencer Cohen Series, Book Three

The Spencer Cohen Series, Yanni's Story

Blood & Milk

The Weight Of It All

A Very Henry Christmas (The Weight of It All 1.5)

Perfect Catch

Switched

Imago

Imagines

Imagoes

Red Dirt Heart Imago

On Davis Row

Finders Keepers

Evolved

Galaxies and Oceans

Private Charter

Nova Praetorian

A Soldier's Wish

Upside Down

The Hate You Drink

Sir

Tallowwood

Reindeer Games

The Dichotomy of Angels

Throwing Hearts

Pieces of You - Missing Pieces #1

Pieces of Me - Missing Pieces #2

Pieces of Us - Missing Pieces #3

Lacuna

Tic-Tac-Mistletoe

Bossy

Code Red

Dearest Milton James

Dearest Malachi Keogh

Christmas Wish List

Code Blue

Davo

The Kite

Learning Curve

Merry Christmas Cupid

To the Moon and Back

Second Chance at First Love

Outrun the Rain

Into the Tempest

Touch the Lightning

EWB - Enemies With Benefits

Holiday Heart Strings

Finders Keepers

Galaxies and Oceans

Nova Praetorian

Upside Down

Sir

Tallowwood

Imago

Throwing Hearts

Sixty Five Hours

Taxes and TARDIS

The Dichotomy of Angels

The Hate You Drink

Pieces of You

Pieces of Me

Pieces of Us

Tic-Tac-Mistletoe

Lacuna

Bossy

Code Red

Learning to Feel

Dearest Milton James

Dearest Malachi Keogh

Three's Company

Christmas Wish List

Code Blue

Davo

The Kite

Learning Curve

Merry Christmas Cupid

To the Moon and Back

Second Chance at First Love

Outrun the Rain

Into the Tempest

Touch the Lightning

EWB

SERIES COLLECTIONS:

Red Dirt Heart Series

Turning Point Series

Thomas Elkin Series

Spencer Cohen Series

Imago Series

Blind Faith Series

Missing Pieces Series

The Storm Boys Series

FREE READS:

Sixty Five Hours

Learning to Feel

His Grandfather's Watch (And The Story of Billy and Hale)

The Twelfth of Never (Blind Faith 3.5)

Twelve Days of Christmas (Sixty Five Hours Christmas)

Best of Both Worlds

Translated Titles:

Italian

Fiducia Cieca (Blind Faith)

Attraverso Questi Occhi (Through These Eyes)

Preso alla Sprovvista (Blindside)

Il giorno del Mai (Blind Faith 3.5)

Cuore di Terra Rossa Serie (Red Dirt Heart Series)

Natale di terra rossa (Red dirt Christmas)

Intervento di Retrofit (Elements of Retrofit)

A Chiare Linee (Clarity of Lines)

Senso D'appartenenza (Sense of Place)

Spencer Cohen Serie (including Yanni's Story)

Punto di non Ritorno (Point of No Return)

Punto di Rottura (Breaking Point)

Punto di Partenza (Starting Point)

Imago (Imago)

Imagines

Il desiderio di un soldato (A Soldier's Wish)

Scambiato (Switched)

Tallowwood

The Hate You Drink

Ho trovato te (Finders Keepers)

Cuori d'argilla (Throwing Hearts)

Galassie e Oceani (Galaxies and Oceans)

Il peso di tut (The Weight of it All)

Pieces of You - Missing Pieces 1

FRENCH

Confiance Aveugle (Blind Faith)

A travers ces yeux: Confiance Aveugle 2 (Through These Eyes)

Aveugle: Confiance Aveugle 3 (Blindside)

À Jamais (Blind Faith 3.5)

Cronin's Key Series

Au Coeur de Sutton Station (Red Dirt Heart)

Partir ou rester (Red Dirt Heart 2)

Faire Face (Red Dirt Heart 3)

Trouver sa Place (Red Dirt Heart 4)

Le Poids de Sentiments (The Weight of It All)

Un Noël à la sauce Henry (A Very Henry Christmas)

Une vie à Refaire (Switched)

Evolution (Evolved)

Galaxies & Océans

Qui Trouve, Garde (Finders Keepers)

Sens Dessus Dessous (Upside Down)

La Haine au Fond du Verre (The hate You Drink)

Tallowwood

THAI

Sixty Five Hours (Thai translation)

Finders Keepers (Thai translation)

SPANISH

Sesenta y Cinco Horas (Sixty Five Hours)

Los Doce Días de Navidad

Código Rojo (Code Red)

Código Azul (Code Blue)

Queridísimo Milton James

Queridísimo Malachi Keogh

El Peso de Todo (The Weight of it All)

Tres Muérdagos en Raya: Serie Navidad en Hartbridge

Lista De Deseos Navideños: Serie Navidad en Hartbridge

Feliz Navidad Cupido: Serie Navidad en Hartbridge

Spencer Cohen Libro Uno

Spencer Cohen Libro Dos

Spencer Cohen Libro Tres

Davo

Hasta la Luna y de Vuelta

Venciendo A La Lluvia

En la Tempestad

El Toque del Rayo

Corazón De Tierra Roja

Corazón De Tierra Roja 2

ECB (Enemigos con Beneficios)

CHINESE

Blind Faith

JAPANESE

Bossy

PORTUGUESE

Sessenta e Cinco Horas